I0660990

Before you had gods, before you had time, before you had good and evil, before you had even you, you had dragonkind and the dragons well nigh took over your world. We didn't let them. We couldn't let them because we were here too.

Unlike us, dragons are built for this plane and can live forever. We, on the other hand, live a long time but can't live long breathing human air so are mortal. Now you know why the rumours started when we put the dragons to sleep. We've been siring an army of newborns to secure our existence ever since as time thaws and our hold over them grow thin. The first of the newborns, you know as Adam. Yet how we are to defeat this enemy we still don't know, for cross-dimensional magic doesn't work on dragons. To kill a dragon one has to do it the only way—the earthly way.

Copyright © 2013. Tn Odu. The Phantom Publisher.
Phantom House Books, Nigeria, in conjunction with
Crieatespace PoD, 7290 B. Investment Drive,
Charleston, SC 29418
Copyright © 2000 - 2011, CreateSpace, a DBA of On-
Demand Publishing,
All rights reserved.
ISBN-10: 978-510787-6
ISBN-13: 978-978-51078-7-6
www.phantomhouseafrica.co.nr
[international dialing code] 23481 3954 0895

angels and DRAGONS,

~Beginning Of~

angels

DRAGONS

~urn of ariel~

Urn of Ariel Vol 1

*Y*ou might have felt it that this universe wasn't built for you. In fact, your world is not nearly as old as you think. Your world is a magic place. Magic built everything. It's in your air, land, and sea. The best way to describe it to your kind would be to call it energy. Every plane has its kind of energy. This energy is what binds us. It is what rules us. The energy of your world is frozen—a vast resource untapped and mostly wasted by your kind. Yet only till we put them asleep, could you have what you have now. You owe everything to us. The dragons sleep by the power of Ariel; the power of us who now rule air, land, and sea. But nothing lives forever. Not even us.

ASXRAU Gold Excavation Mine, La Paz, Bolivia

"They are there."

"Do not make them discover it."

"They've already found it."

"Then why are they still there?"

"They are as resilient as we are. It's a good sign."

"—they are stubborn. Seal it!"

The disparity in their number of wings and not the colour of their corporeal form told who had the power of say and who had to obey. It also told which angel was in government. Apparently, none were.

Eae bore four wings, not that his wings could be seen by the naked eye, so he commanded Mihr to seal off the mine. It'd be the 6th time they did so in the last six centuries, guarding the gates to Eden—every century harbouring at least one insect with dreams of making history and reining in the Armageddon whether conscious of it or not.

One of the miners struck what seemed to be a shiny new ore at the fronts, but it didn't budge. He tried to chisel into it, but it even dented his chisel. The boys called in the diamond tipped drill but that didn't work either. The rocks seemed of polished lustre and formed a sagacious pattern about the tributary. "Tell the boss we've stumbled on something!" hollered the miner to the others down the mine shaft.

"If you say their rise is inevitable, why not we save the 500 mining down there instead? Six is not a good number, but five certainly is," she suggested, but Eae's eyes glowered red—that's when the slight tremors kicked in and a fault slipped. The mine's tributaries yielded to the superimposed weight of the rocks above and Asxrau buried itself beneath 1050ft of rock. Along with it, 500 mine workers.

Jason Ketuga. East London, South Africa

E very stormy night, all year round, Jason Ketuga encounters the silhouette of a man he's never met in his dreams. The man doesn't do anything, but watch him sleep through the storm. Most of his face is

shadowed off, even when it thunders, but the reason Jason remembers each dream is the ever-present imprint of wings when the lightning hits—four black wings for the black silhouette.

"And you say you see this man when you sleep, Mr. Ketuga?" the hypnotist asked again before proceeding with the session. Just to be sure.

"Yes," Jason replied succinctly with a homely Afrikaans accent, one common with those saved from growing urban culture.

"And you say you never grew up with your father, Mr. Ketuga."

"No."

"Would you say you could recognize his face if you ever saw him again?"

"What's this? Com'on doctor. It's not like i don't see him every now and then. Of course i would," he gibed.

"I don't mean pictures, Mr. Ketuga."

There was a large collection of ink paintings to a side of the doctor's suburbanian office. "Do you see his face—the man in your dreams?" the hypnotist asked, as he leaned Jason into the recliner sofa and set one of the ink paintings before him. He was an elderly man but not too old.

"No," Jason answered tensely, unsure what the picture was for. It looked like a painting of a bedroom.

"I want you to relax your mind and just focus on this picture," the old hypnotist advised and drew up a stool by Jason's side to sit on. "Are you sure you do not see his face?" he asked again, and suddenly Jason could hear a light ticking. He wasn't sure if the sound was stemming from the old man's watch, being that they now held hands, or the clock resting idly across the wall. He wasn't even sure his eyes were still open. But certainly, he could feel the coldness and loud thundering of last night's storm. Everything looked as black as ink in his bedroom, save the blue flashes coming from behind his window curtains. The man with no face was also there, outlined in the darkness of his bedroom as always, his silhouette watching intently. This time around, however, Jason had companionship in the darkness, "Do you see his face?" the hypnotist asked, his voice able to reach inside Jason's head.

"No," Jason replied before attempting to approach the silhouette in the darkness. It was the first of any action he'd ever taken in his dreams of the stranger, but that was when two red dots peered at him from the darkness, "I do not see his face, but I see his eyes. They are red eyes," he answered briskly.

"Is he angry then? May be with someone? May be with you?" the hypnotist asked suggestively and Jason sighed no. "I don't feel any anger. Just inertness," he answered, but on getting close enough to touch the stranger, Jason flinched—and not just in his dreams.

"Why did you flinch, Mr. Ketuga?" the old man inquired tenderly only for the man outlined in the darkness to get

on both feet. They had been pretty long feet and he towered to the ceiling, staring down at Jason. His eyes red as crimson and focused.

"Fuck me, he's big," Jason whispered off plumb.

"Don't stray Mr. Ketuga, you need to follow the sound of my voice. And no vulgar expressions if you please. Why did you flinch?"

"I flinched because he has black wings," Jason answered honestly, "but I only see them when the lightning flashes."

"Do his wings scare you, Mr. Ketuga? Is he trying to frighten you? Bully you into submission?"

"No," Jason answered, again honestly, "he's just looking at me."

"Then you are not afraid of him. If you're not afraid of him what is it you want to say to him? Isn't that why you are here, Mr. Ketuga?"

"I came here because I want to see his face—and because my friends promised they'd refund my money if you were a coocoo bird," Jason answered as flat as a spade, unable to put a lid on his candour. He even made a smile despite the trance.

"My profession is not a game, Jason. Neither am I—what you call it—a coocoo bird. Now, I want you to boldly ask him to step into the light. If there is no light in there with you, Jason, find some lights and put them on."

But Jason didn't need to and woke up from the trance in haste. "Wow," he said and was on his feet, "this was more engaging than I thought, Dr. Mc Callaghan. How do you do it—?"

"Did you see his face?" the hypnotist interrupted, trying to return his train of thought.

"No," Jason lied and grabbed whatever was left of his belongings in the small office overlooking the ocean.

"Colour plays a very important role in our subconscious minds. Visions of red eyes, black wings, form and shapes of demons, everything plays an important role when projecting your alter ego into the living person—" Dr. Mc Callaghan lectured.

Jason didn't wait. He just walked out. Actually, he did the good doctor a favour paying by the hour.

1050.20ft of rubble was what was left of the Asxrau gold mine and atop the dragon that lay asleep inside its stone prison. A black hexagram crowned with numbers marked its position upon the site but vanished as quickly as it appeared. Another angel was coming, but not just any angel, the seal of Solomon of Solomon went before the record keepers. This angel played politics. Eae returned his eyes to the eyes of the everyday Caucasian sycophant, the cherub was bedecked in strapping pants and a sly chambray vest, but Mihr stiffened at the sight. She was clad simply in army green denim overall. The lucifugous seraph appeared in plain glory—six wings without charm, each winging out in plain sight and three times a foot long except for the lumbar wings—the in-betweens always a feet or two shorter and usually flagging around the body. His burnished charbroiled skin was obvious to no one in the shade, since there was no longer a soul on site.

The dark angel had a voice that travelled with the wind, it seemed to boom everywhere, "this will go into their records, apprentice. It wouldn't be long before other humans are here with their cameras."

"I will take care of their records," Eae answered obsequiously, and on behalf of Mihr. She did all the work being his apprentice.

"That won't be necessary—the urn is gone. Ariel has returned," he said gravely and his words fell like an elephant to the ground. Both angels had a textbook lecture of the proper response to when the waiting was up, but there the apprentices stood unresponsive.

"Where are we to gather, Ouriel?" Eae responded finally.

"We do not gather. It's been decided. Go anywhere but here," the seraph answered when the ground broke and a hand clawed out of it. There was a worker still alive. He looked traumatized and his face was all but a little part covered in dirt and dust, still the worker was able to acknowledge the winged difference between the dark-skinned gentleman and the other two in his company, "buchara! No quiero morir ahora," he cried on spotting the black wings hanging lightly in the air.

15

The seraph didn't bother to hide his wings, "take care of this one. Find the urn if you can, but leave this place," he instructed vanishing with a crack of thunder.

"Do what Ouriel says," the cherub instructed his apprentice and Mihr floated over to help the survivor a good degree off the rumble. Mihr glowed like the moon around people so it was commonplace for him to worship her. He prayed obediently, chanting his rosary offhandedly to her, which made her decide to pluck him completely out of the dirt and sing to him. She sang to him, singing in rhyme and seducing his body to give off a hazy evanescence of some sort. It came off him and into her completely when she laid her hands on his head, and a tear fell down her eye. The ground tremors resumed when his body fell peacefully to the ground. She looked to Eae. "That's not me," the cherub confessed as the entire site cracked beneath their feet and Mihr fell to the ground. She'd lost her suspension. More rocks cracked open and all four of Eae's wings came into open view. Same thing had happened to both her wings. She looked as puzzled as he was. "That's not me again," the cherub confessed a second time. He shoved her and set her running as more rocks gave way to fire and brimstone. "Get out of here!"

"What about you?" she inquired neither having the time nor balance to look back at the cherub.

"Just go!" he bellowed at her angrily. The entire site collapsed into the ground just when she nicked the periphery of its vent and an intense luminous wall of molten rock and fire erupted out of it. She was only able

to teleport when she'd tumbled off the plateau and into the trees. By the time she woke, wherever she woke, the sulphur had nicked her heels and it bled a black viscous liquid. It was the first time in her brief eternity of a life that Mihr sustained an injury. Or learned of her animate mortality. She shed another tear, but it was not for the life she had taken.

A/1C Teresa Xixo. Kimberly Plateaux. Near Fort Nelson.

Only two Albatrosses course the airzone over Kimberly. Both wingmen fly in echelon and fly fast. "This is Alba 4 -5. Alba 4-5 to Alba 2-2. Earth to Trixie. It's just a routine flyby baby," the pilot shot through the intercom when he flashed by her.

"Yeah—thanks for reminding me. Mind was somewhere else," Teresa answered mindlessly, adjusting her MiG to the fly zone.

"And what's bothering my chocolate beauty today?—I bet you five rands i can put my finger on it. Two words—boy trouble. FYI, you know I can always help you with that," he teased and she laughed into the intercom.

"Yeah Charlie. I have boy trouble and you're the first boy i ask for help," she taunted.

"What can I say but that I love chocolate?"

Both MiGs picked up a blip on the radar. "I'm picking up a M6-24 Drop Bird on radar, but we are freshly out of those

I'm guessing, so what gives?—I know its HUC's maintenance week. Alba 2-2 what's your reading?"

"All is good from what I'm reading, but you know this equipment. Sometimes they see shit! Best get a visual."

"Visual in sight," Charles answered and called it in, "This is Alba 4-5 to HQ; we have a size M6-24 Drop Bird on radar. What's her status?"

"No friendlies in the vicinity. You are at green light to intercept," the intercom responded and both MiGs engaged gear near supersonic speed, only to observe what appeared as a visible blotch in the radar steadily grow bigger.

"2-2, do you have a visual of the Drop Bird?" he asked Trixie and she affirmed him.

"No, but what the fuck is it?" she asked back, nervously.

"We're soon to find out. Unidentified Flying Object, this is South African Air Patrol Albatross U2-4-1Routineer and you're in restricted airspace. Identify yourself and wait to be escorted to Fort Nelson or you will be shot down," Charlie had warned the big blue dot in the radar.

"Alba 4-5 to HQ, requesting permission to engage."

"Alba 4-5, you're at green light to engage," came back the response and Charlie launched a T21 directly at it and the missile exploded on impact, but that was when they heard it thunder—a hollow and reverberating roar. The small bomb didn't even slow it down a sec. Whatever it was and

then they saw coming their way in the blink of an instant. It appeared to flap wings.

"I don't think that's a Drop Bird," Teresa announced and they hightailed out of its way as it flew past them, but not fast enough as a scaly green and granite-hard chalcedony tail whisked by and knocked both Albatrosses out of the air. Charlie took first impact. He died from the explosion in the air and not when the Albatross hit the ground. Trixie took second impact. Her equipments running wildly was all she could remember when the MiG spun violently out of control, broke apart, and exploded on crashing into the trees and rocks below.

T he world goes to hell," Jason Ketuga said while watching the news. Someone had been murdered—a member of council or something, but he wasn't sure if the following headline he saw was really live footage or just some hoax by a rather skilful animator. Everything was perfect. All the shadows were in place. Still whatever it was, that certainly wasn't a dragon burning native Bolivians to a crisp now, was it? Hell, what were they thinking putting up such kid stuff on international TV? A light boom followed and the live footage lost its feed or went off air.

"Did you get that?" Jason asked the barman who switched the tube to the ball channel.

"I'd rather watch this," the barman replied without concern, wiping down a number of small drinking glasses.

He asked for a refill. "Who won the game?"

"Which game?"

"You know—that game?"

"You mean the nations cup game?—shit, Nigeria won 2 nil. The fuckers!" he spat tastelessly and sought to refill Jason's cup of morning black.

"Not to worry, we'll get them next time."

The live feed came back on. The higher ups had interrupted the soccer channel. Only this time it was a very different camera, and it didn't look like Bolivia. In fact, it looked much closer to home.

"Do you get what's up with this?" Jason asked and the barman fingered at the TV.

"That's us. That's sun city," he stated emphatically and the dude popped out his computer phone. The same feed was streaming from it, and he showed it to Jason. The public servant was confused. It showed a straight chain of destruction, even right past the great stadium, which was in flames and ruins. "What's the pointer for?" he inquired of the arrow blinking right above the screens.

"That's the compass—shows it's headed here."

"What's headed here?"

"Beats me," he answered succinctly when Jason noticed his cup of coffee black ripple out on occasion.

The barman was a chubby man, but his look was same as Jason's—flushed pink and slowly spooked out.

The ripples became vibrations, and the vibrations became thunder, but he didn't wait for the tremors to hit before he and the barman took for the exits. Upon getting safely outside, it seemed like evening as he watched a castle-wide creature blank out the sun for a moment and fighter jets scrambling by. It looked like a moving planet from beneath and the jets bombarded it ferociously. That was the thundering sound. Still, the giant flying planet of a beast didn't look even perturbed by the assault from the military.

"You must be shitting me," the barman muttered when he came out from around the back of the pub. He hit record on his computer phone.

"I don't believe it," Jason remarked and watched it fly a direct course towards the sea. The whole city was abuzz, and everyone who didn't run away, loot property, or seek shelter was out in the open scared shitless. But, that was not all Jason saw. Only this time, he was certain it wasn't a dream being broad daylight and a startling 12:13. A winged shadow of a man soared across the ground and buildings. Apparently, headed for the sea as well.

He looked to the sky and sun but couldn't find anything in the air that cast down such a large shadow, despite the fact the shadow was cast boldly, as present as it was moving over cars, people and buildings. Jason grabbed the barman by the shoulder but the barman reacted unkindly, he too was more than spooked out, "what the—"

"Do you see that?" Jason went ahead to ask.

"Of course I fucking see that—I'm not blind. It's a freaking dragon! The fucker!"

"No," Jason tugged at the man's collar, "I meant the shadow. Keep your eye on the shadow," he pointed towards the freaking large impression of a man with wings cast over the buildings as it went along.

"What shadow?" the barman rejoined.

"You don't see it?"

He shouldered off Jason's hands. "There's no fucking shadow," he snorted and returned to the safety of his pub. The huge planet of a beast plunged several miles out into the open sea despite the efforts of the SA Navy who had been launching surface to air missiles at it. Or the air jets who'd reconned the area firing air to ground missiles after it. The resulting tsunami wretched a ship and ate a little into the coastline with minimal damage to public infrastructure. Nobody could stop it. In actual fact nobody could see it, but Jason. The notary hopped into an abandoned vehicle. Why he was stealing this property, he had no answer. All he had was this tightening feeling in the pit of his gut.

The humans were unable to stop it. Belamir's headed for the pit. It's not gunning for the urn."

"Then do what must be done."

"It's already done."

The seraphs in the sky watched the cherubs and angels in the sea, of those rebellious enough to gather and attempt one last stand, stand side by side with the legion of mermen to fortify the perimeter bordering hell's cove; an army of monstrous octopuses and giant sharks actually intended to keep the humans away. It wasn't at all disconcerting to see them wanting to prove the legends false. Over a hundred thousand years of wilful employment can do that to any being, but this particular dragon had eyes like a cat, and a jutting organ for a horn, growing not on its colossal head but rather under its shovel of a jaw when it came plunging into the cold water sea like a colossal meteorite. It came in a beeline for the pit swimming towards the ocean bottom in a vortex clocking 150 km/hr. The legend was true. They could do nothing to resist because their magic failed, and just when the planet of a beast was close enough to be struck. The vortex sucked everyone in—swallowing all caught in its grip down under. A good number lost their hold over energy and awkwardly transformed into people folk, with neither gills nor flippers to keep from drowning. They drowned within a sub tide of its wings and fell as pillars of salt to the ocean bottom, their urns eviscerating in solution. On the other hand, the planet of a beast had gills to breathe underwater and its hard scaled wings attached to its body served as fins for the dive. It hadn't forgotten the channel to hell's cove as it smashed through the reinforced rocks and ores the made the inner perimeter of hell cove. It all happened so quickly. Of everything, only the animals escaped, making their way to freedom free of the hold of their pretenatural masters.

It was a battle of no contest. And Samuel watched it from the air, watching alongside the Sanhedrin of seraphs. "They failed," he stated matter-of-factly. "It is as she predicted."

"It was agreed not any would gather until we can find Ariel," Raphael protested tenderly. Her energy was of the earth, giving a rich glow to her pale brown form.

"We did," Samuel responded unmoved, "Now we've lost 200 before even the battle has begun." Each seraph was inexpressive, not encumbered by grief or emotions, as they should be in times like these.

They watched the air jets fly by them on reconnaissance and the strange whirlpool about the sea's surface. The Royal Navy and two US Navy submarines also surfaced amidst the passel of warships, safely away from the vortex. "They do their best," Zaphiel counselled in the unseen gathering of five and seven. His was a fiery visage.

"They do what they can," Samuel responded flatly. "The time has come to do what we agreed. The coming century is lean so we cannot gather. We do not gather. We do not fight. It's their war now not ours."

"They won't survive by themselves," Raphael protested but everyone else sheltered their wings and disappeared. "If they don't survive, we die! You said it yourself, they are only as frail as we are!" she cracked at them and her eyes flashed red only for a storm to develop out in the open sea

venting her rage. She had to leave and not interfere with the ships or air jets. The humans didn't need her muddling things up. What they needed, however, was all the help they could get for what was coming out of the depths of hell's cove.

For over an hour and a half, Trixie lay passed out within the trees. She'd hit the eject button by muscle memory, but her life she owed to the cushion of twigs and branches that broke her fall and caught her parachute. The problem she had now was how to free herself from the 20ft tree without dying. There stood a stronger branch right across from her, but it was too far to reach and quite the wild card. Still, Trixie fumbled for her penknife and went to work on each of the belts securing her to the parachute. She cut loose two belts and tried swinging for the branch, but it didn't work. Whatever stunt she'd attempted to pull off, it didn't matter when the twigs snapped and her parachute tore free of its grip. She tumbled the full 20 feet and snapped a vertebra with the force with which she hit the buttress root across the forest floor. Trixie couldn't feel a thing shoulder down, feeling faint and ever more tired with each passing second she lay helpless. A red pentagram with numbers marked the tree before her but disappeared as quickly and it appeared her mind was beginning to play tricks. The entire jungle grew blurry and wonky very quickly. Yet, the light that brought Mihr falling into the jungle was one hard to miss. She hadn't displayed her wings and could barely walk properly when she got up, but more stood out to the stranger than a dirty face and the simple denim overall she was wearing.

Mihr sought to walk on by when she noticed Trixie flat against her back helpless with her life ebbing away, but Trixie called to her, "help. Help me. Please help!"

Mihr squatted by the dying pilot. The angel needed to find treatment for her bleeding foot. "I know what it feels like now to be wounded, but I can make the pain go away. I can make this easier for you," she offered tenderly and placed a hand over the black girl's head. But the girl, writhing in pain, stubbornly fought her hands off by wriggling her head.

"No help. I said i need you to help me. Help me."

There was death in her voice, but something else as well—defiance. Something about the first airman desperately fought for life. Mihr leaned over her and looked into her eyes, "where are you from?" she asked softly.

"Fort Nelson. SAAP Routineer," Trixie cited bravely, fading more with every breath she forced.

Mihr looked deeper into her eyes, "No. I want you to tell me where you are from, Trixie?" she asked again.

"Namaqualand, Springbok," she answered and her eyes dilated upon noticing two swanned wings towering over her like a canopy.

"You see my wings because you are dying, Teresa of Springbok. If I give you your life back, you must know it belongs to me. Are you willing to trade me your life—"

"Just fucking help me please," Trixie answered before the angel could finish as a hazy mist seeped out of the ground and clung avariciously to the tough biscuit.

"Then I name you my apprentice Teresa of Springbok," Mihr pronounced and imprinted her finger across the head of the first airman, not sure such an imprint would work on a human being such a fragile existent. The young angel was breaking every rule in place. She wasn't even near old enough to have an apprentice. And according to the extent of her knowledge, no human was ever named so. It was energy highly unstable and not channelled for this plane, but this was her choice and could possibly be her last shot at this if their time was up.

Trixie felt energy imbue her bones and her vertebrae lock in place as the haziness seeped back into the ground. But the green imprint remained ever glowing across her forehead, it was supposed to disappear after taking effect. There was something definitely different about this airman. Something different enough to have Mihr worried.

A storm was brewing over the sea as Jason steered his stolen pickup truck along the coastline. It was leaking gas, but the notary didn't know that. All he knew was he that had a good view of everything happening out at sea, and if he continued at this pace, he'd probably stumble into Port Edward without realizing it. The whirlpool subsided only to give way to a lot of bubbling and intense activity. The colossal planet of a beast was nowhere to be seen, only for a staggering roar to emanate from the waters having Jason almost run into incoming traffic. A flight of dragons took to the darkening clouds in more numbers than anyone could count, none as big as the first but all able to spit fire or something at the air jets that flew their way. The military had sought to engage, but that was until the dragons in the water emerged and the military realized that was not a tactical plan. They were outnumbered probably a score to one, and of the water dragons, some had their dorsal fins larger than the US naval submarines on standby, so they revised that plan. More jets and ships came, but none of the dragons had the intention of staying. All the water dragons swam away while those in the air flew away under a billow of fire and smoke. The one that stayed, the only one shot down by one of airjets, was the one to worry about. The red dragon came crashing down into the roadway ahead, and Jason veered the pickup off the road to keep from crashing into it. Apparently, it was a small dragon, the runt of the litter, and possibly the reason the military had shot it down. It had a snake forked tongue and landed on all fours. It expanded its horn-tipped wings to find the impression of a missile right through it, and at that moment something told the notary to hightail his way out of the highway—the red demon harboured a grudge. Jason made an absolute 180 and hit the gas as the dragon lifted itself off the ground and spat a viscous translucent liquid at the very jet that brought it down. The solution ate through the locomotive in seconds and the pilot and his craft crashed into the highway in pieces. But, that wasn't all. Apparently the small dragon could read numbers. It picked off the fighter jets one by one, and serially, deftly outmanoeuvring their heat missiles until there was no longer a locomotive in the air, or sea, as it shrewdly manoeuvred the heat seeking missiles to the warships and submarines in the water. The flying beast vented whatever was left of its vengeance on all the locomotives on the highway running the coastline, spiting acid while launching other vehicles into the sea. It reached for Jason's truck, but the notary saw it coming through the rear view mirror long before it came for him and took a dive out the driver's seat. It tossed the truck clear over him but the vehicle exploded like a small bomb before it could toss it out to sea, so it came after Jason. And the city he ran into.

ood god. Thank you for saving me."

"Don't thank me if god is what you think i am. I am not your god."

"But you're an angel, aren't you? A guardian angel."

"I see you see me as intriguing, but know now I am no one's messenger."

"What are you but not a messenger?" Trixie asked, a bit confused, not able to take her eyes off the two broad wings tightly-folded into Mihr's back.

The angel made her wings disappear into her denim overall to cut down the airman's boorish staring, "It is sufficient that i am different from you." Mihr had her face cleaned up and hair pulled back. "You're my apprentice now, Teresa of Springbok. I rescued you for a reason. You will have no other choice but to do whatever i will."

"Always?" Trixie asked back.

"Yes, always. Or you will lose that mark and most certainly die," Mihr stated matter-of-factly and got on her feet.

It was amazing to watch her appear so ordinary. "I hear you. I want to thank you for saving me anyway. I do not know your name? What should i call you?"

"Mihr."

"Thank you Mihr. Where is it you're heading?"

"I am on a quest, Teresa of Springbok. My quest is the reason is the reason you're coming with me. It'll be less dangerous for your kind than mine so I'll be needing assistance."

"You healed me, so why not heal yourself? You're bleeding, aren't you? And the name's Trixie," she replied between one too many questions, everly curious as humans were.

Mihr turned to her bleeding foot, "I've never been wounded before...Teresa of Springbok," the angel retorted obstinately, "and this is wound I cannot heal for reasons you do not understand."

The first airman looked confused, so Mihr looked into Trixie's moist maple eyes to clear her reasoning, "I know you've seen it, Teresa of Springbok. I've seen you see it. You see it now, don't you?"

"What is it?—that thing that killed my partner?"

"What you saw we know as Belamir. Belamir's been asleep for years. The seraphs hid them until today. They've been here longer than any of us."

"Them? They?—you're saying there's more like that thing somewhere out there?"

"Not just somewhere—Hell's Cove, a place frozen in time. The elders watched the earth swallow them whole when they slipped through the portal, but the belamir you saw killed your friend they imprisoned away from Hell's Cove. He's of a different kind."

"So what do you want this Belamir? He is what you're going after, isn't he Mihr?" Teresa asked, feeling quite stronger and braver than she usually felt. But how she expressly came to know the answer to that by just looking Mihr in the eye was what intrigued her, "you want the urn of Ariel," the former pilot dictated instinctively, startled by the sudden openness of her mind.

more jets were waiting back at the city with missiles armed and ready. He'd brought danger back to the port city. They fired on sight, and just in the nick of time before the red dragon could run Jason to the ground and claw him off the asphalt. It crashed clean through a building but emerged angrier, spitting acid at everything flying overhead, after which it spotted Jason running for the Metro and derailed a train just to intercept him. "What the fuck did i do to you?" Jason protested, his shirt and tie on the fly as it blocked off the inlet to the subway. It came for him but military tanks launched a bazooka at it tossing it five yards across the road and clear through a brick wall. Yet, it bounced back like a rubber toy using highway cars as a platform to launch itself back into the air. More airjets riddled it with bullets hoping to lure it away from the city and Jason used the moment to escape down to the subway.

"Look Mister! I don't know what you did, but you don't bring your shit down here!" a man had threatened at the end of the flight of stairs. He had a brick in hand.

"You better be ready to kill me because I'm coming down there!" Jason shot back, only to discover he was live on television and it was more than apparent he was what the red beast was gunning for. There was a whole city of people down the subway. "Stay the fuck away! You want to meet my friend?" he threatened the whole crowd, trying his best to keep all of them at arm's length, though more scared than the face he put up. He could hear his heart beating and feel the blood piping through his arteries, his body on the brink of panic. Jason secured an entire bleacher to himself since everyone in the subway wanted to stay as clear off him as they possibly could, but had barely had time to sit and breathe when he recognized a familiar face in the crowd evenly trying to put a distance between them. He left the bleachers and

went after her, losing her to the crowd on occasion but always able to finger her out again. He'd lost her for the final time when he got to a huge vending machine with broken lights.

"Shit!"

He was frustrated and in desperate need of some answers when the red dragon crashed through the bricks and reinforced concrete into the subway, intense and steamed over. "You must be shitting me," Jason stated, and the hysteria in the subway hit the fan. How it could figure him from the crowd was rudimentary. The dragon viciously emptied the subway, running into folks and melting people, thinning out the crowd by the minute as it tried to fly properly in the limited space of a subway when a fierce hand grabbed Jason and arrested him behind the dispenser.

"How are you doing this? I have changed into four men still you come after me—what are you?"

She stood a pale Indo-Aryan lady in black trench coat threatening him with an empty hand.

"Four men? What the fuck are you talking about, woman?" Jason panicked, frightened to shit for being trapped in a subway with a killer dragon and no escape route.

She forced him to the ground with no difficulty whatsoever, her hand still over his head, "how is it you know I'm female?—who are you? Why are you after me?"

"I didn't figure you'd be woman. I see your face in my dreams. I only wanted to know why," Jason retorted and tried to lift himself off her grip when her eyes flashed red and her supposedly empty hand yielded a glass spear that extended to pinch his throat. He lay back on the ground as she watched him. Apparently she was hell of a lot stronger than he could ever be.

She sought to test him. "If you can see into me, then you can see my wings," she said suggestively, and right away he saw it—six impression of wings spanning out in glory. They were there but again not really there, looking less like feathers and more like human hair, even as darkening nerves materialized about her face before reverting to her pale indo-Aryan form.

"What are you?" Jason asked back and the question took her by surprise.

"You're Nephilim! I should run you through," she threatened and pinched him again with her spear when the spear disappeared all by itself and the red dragon knocked the dispenser away. It had found them, and stabbed her in the shoulder with its horn-tipped wing. She bled. Her blood was black as ink and strangely healed the dragon's all but handicapped wings by the second.

She had answers so Jason picked up a loose 10 inch screw from behind the vending machine and bravely stabbed the red dragon in the eye with it, pulling her away from its grip. It also bled black but his entire arm hurt. He'd never touched anything that hard before, and neither had anything that hard touched him—with just one swing of

its wing, it knocked him out of its way and into the
concrete half blind. The notary could barely breathe.
Raphael homed in on the other eye with another glass
spear, but the spear broke instantly and disintegrated into
nothing whilst the wound she inflicted healed almost
instantaneously. It stabbed into her with its horn-tipped
wings, fastening her in place, repairing itself, and
preparing to spit her down when Jason pushed her out of
the way and it spat all over him. The military dropped a
small bomb in the subway. They probably realized it was
now empty and the shooting recommenced. The smoke
bomb was to flush it out, which it did. They came in with
dragnets, gas masks and night vision. In the end, they
didn't find anyone in the rumble aside the community of
corpses the dragon had left in its wake.

H ell's Cove now had two exits, as the planet of a beast
broke through the rocks and ores but remained under
water heading a new course and heading south. The
gilled dragon didn't surface, and not once, as it moved
beneath the seas swimming for days and evading sonar.
Each bleep from a vessel or submarine was like music in
the water. It avoided contact. Aside the fact, the humans
were not the only ones searching for it. It could also hear
it—telepathy—that's how best to describe the other kind
of music. The angels weren't the only ones searching for
the urn. The urn of Ariel made a strange kind of music, a
new melody of vibration, only the beast could hear. It
called to the planet of a beast, seducing it and drawing it
closer, drawing it in—a melody beyond what it could
resist. The dragon only burst forth at the Southern Alps

after swimming around the entire continent of Australia. There a pillar of salt was waiting at the mouth of a mountain pass, frozen solid with the rest of the ice and much intact. It had found the urn and the dragon imbibed the urn whole. The dragon's eyes switched yellow, red, and back again and there it made its first call to the other males after a hundred thousand years of sleeping—a call as loud as a clarion and yet as silent as a dog's whistle. Not even the angels heard it.

*S*ave the wings, we almost look alike. You look just like us. It's why there are cherubim who believe what the seraphim preach. That your kind will balance out the war. They believe in it so blindly, they are willing to take a chance with your kind. It's the reason we built Mesopotamia and the first city. But after your little stunt at Babel, the rest of us just look to your kind for distraction and amusement. You are as frail as we are, in your own way. Even worse, you can't work magic.

Rio Muni, Gulf of Guinea, 1944

Dónde vas, señor?" the man behind the oars asked out loud, his sombrero half out to save his face from Africa's yellow sun, "yo pregunto porque no lo conozco los barrios propiamente," he lied. The lanky officer to whom he was addressing wore an uncommon grey uniform and a priggish black hat. He wasn't alone and had a fly whisk to swat bugs and mosquitoes off his face.

The commandant mumbled something in German to the other officers in two similar canoes piloted by slave merchants, before checking his compass. All six officers were priggishly dressed. "Keep going that way," he pointed and secured his feet against an arm of the canoe. They were headed the right direction and thicker into the swamp.

"El Alemano tomanos para tontos. No voy para negocios. You no find slave there. We no find slaves here," he remarked in pidgin. Not only that, his disappointment sounded infectious; infectious enough to cause the commandant to frown. But rather than frown, the commandant beamed at the fellow, pointing out his swastika and a wad of cash. They were things of honour. "Get me there and I pay double," he tossed the money to the merchant and the fellow grinned fondly, but then hesitated in taking the money.

"no quiero morir hoy, señor Goering. Mis compañeros también. No pueden tomarlos allí."

"So you do know where we're going?" Goering remarked and smiled at him. "I was beginning to think it a fool's errand."

"se Diablo vive allí, señor. Nadie vas allí y volvas," he demurred, but the commandant's patience had run out. The same way he pulled a pistol out. So did his fellow officers. "You honour our agreement or in the name of the fuehrer I will spatter your brains all over this boat—as well as your fellow traders," he threatened, and so the merchant stirred his canoe along the meandering course for the rest of the journey without as much as an objection. After an hour and after directing the merchant into the mangrove, he ordered everyone off.

"but senor?"

"Who's going to get us back, boatman? You better not fall off," he sneered, referring to the swamp and water snakes about the place.

His officers did the rest. All the merchants came off and clambered over the sturdy prop roots deeper and deeper into the mangrove forest for minutes on end, led by the commandant until they reached stone-cut rocks. The mangrove had grown into large basaltic rocks, only to reveal an abandoned city of stone shielded from the sea and the outside world by deep forest mangrove.

The slave merchants took off their sombreros, "madre del dios."

The entire city and even its flooring were made from gigantic uncut stones—immovable by any technology, almost as if it was sculptured in place. And aside the evergreen life of creeping plants and moss growing along its cracks and walls, it stood a despondent creation of purely volcanic rock.

The commandant cheered at the sight and the Germans holstered their pistols. They congratulated one another. "Okay, keep moving!" he flagged the merchants to proceed into the city. There stood two towering statues of angels, one visibly lighter, and the other darker, despite all the weathering and decay, and each having six wings obscuring their eyes, their nipples and their privates. The monuments were so large, they stood visible from any angle of the city.

River water feed the city from the right, through what appeared to be a complex network of irrigation channels. And despite the blotch of a water fountain that had fallen, breaking up a few of the channels and flooding a little over half the city whilst leaving the other half as parched as a desert, it all stood gallantly. Beautifully elevated walkways connected everything.

"los diablos vive alli," a few of the merchants spoke, their voices trembling, repeating the solo over and over as they wandered through the city until they got the Germans feeling uneasy and the officers reintroduced their pistols. "What are your companions saying?" the commandant asked his boatman with gun in hand. After all, he was spokesman for all three slave merchants.

"It's what I be telling you. They say Devil lives here. This is sacred place," he answered snappishly.

The German sneered. They avoided the water and headed for the center edifice, being the biggest and grandest structure in sight. Everything else was built around it, and apparently for it. They rolled up like flies at the portico of its entrance, its colonnade being so huge. All the columns inside the giant dome structure were uncut. And with tiers centering down to a huge chasm, this imposing edifice stood out a city of its own. A work of god.

"Madre sagrado! What is this place?" the merchant asked on looking down the chasm. There were at least two more cities like the one they were in still visible, each with its own columns and tiers, in levels centered down the chasm. The rest lay wholly submerged underwater from some dysfunction from the channels.

The commandant tacked up a smirk. "Didn't think you saw all of it, did you?" he cheered. "It is the city inside the city, the tower of Babel, built for giants," the German remarked, referring to the legends, "with what we will

44

scavenge from this place, we will be able to turn around this war! The fuehrer will be most pleased!" In his exclamation, his voice echoed throughout the giant dome and down to the cities below.

"Then we must begin at once, Herr Goering. I do not think the fuehrer will be able to hold off the allied forces if we do not return in time. We left Auschwitz under heavy bombardment," one of the other Germans suggested, seeking to remind his commandant of the circumstances surrounding their visit. Yet, the mere mention of it was sufficient to light up the commandant like a matchstick.

"It is treason to speak that. Speak of it again I will put a bullet in your head, Kamerad Viktor!" the commandant threatened, and about the time one of the slave merchants took to flight after spotting something or pointing at someone. "bruchera!" he had pronounced before the commandant put a bullet in him. "Nobody leaves!" he yelled, even aiming the pistol at his own officers. There was no one else around the entire site outside the company of eight, plus one; the dead one. The dead man's blood highlighted a detailed maze of engravings and symbols across the floor and when the commandant realized what it was, asked his fellow officers to provide him a lighter. It was oil—there was oil asides the blood. The hombres handed him the match instead, everyone equally curious as he set it alit. The carvings lit up the entire place in a subtle copper flame as the ancient city came alive. It had runes and hieroglyphs on how the city was built from ground up, symbols of a's, s's and x's, etched, scratched, and re-etched in the worship of perfect circles.

"There are only six cities, but not quite like this one, all over the world," the commandant mentioned to his compeers, "one on each continent—of course Europe and Asia all counts as one big continent even if the fools deceive themselves otherwise," he remarked, in a mood for a little laugh. "Same could be said of the Americas. Of the six, we are in the surviving one. Unless you see it fit we travel to the South Pole. I, on the other hand believe Africa is much friendlier," he said, referring to the merchants and their slave labour, and his compeers laughed.

"But this is not what we come for. Many others dismissed this place as legend, but the legends prove true. And they say the first city has six gates, each gate a doorway to the one true city. A city with great and unseen power! Legends say not ever before seen, but now, with our finding this, I say not ever again. This is Babel, meine kameraden. We are at the city to that city. Hiel Hitler!"

Keneji Jamidi, Babel, West Africa [8700BC]

It was not always 6 cities but six havens. Each haven towering side by side to the haven of angels and each assigned a custodian. Jamidi of the Gulf was custodian of Babel, haven of the black race, yet for all his wives, he had one son, Keneji of the Jamidi given to him by the gods for a price of worth. The monarchy was temporary, constantly on rotation, with the calendar coming to a close of the Jamidi Year, and soon enough, the onset of the Amakii, the year another royal family took up office and a

different capital administered the great tower for a cycle of a 1461 days. The custodian's unique drive this cycle was infrastructure, and social welfare, available to the thronging masses that lived in the great city—and that would be Eae's cue. It was a city spanning the heavens after all, for in the beginning humankind never had to exhaust the earth to live on it.

"The offering is half-price?"

"You're welcome to take it for a spin before you buy, Your Highness."

It was just too good to be true. Nobody sold a saucer half price and everyone had good reason to be skeptical about such new tech, which was also the reason the merchant was the only one remaining at the trading port all morning. But now, with his intending buyer being son of the custodian, Eae could foretell how the rest of this negotiation would go.

"The offering is half price?" the young prince reiterated and Eae beamed back at the young, black and vibrant teen royal. Eae too was of black form, even if his corporeal impression blanketed his one true form. For as it was, Babel was a multicultural city, stretching ground under and towering sky high with her gates open for trade every day and round the clock. Aside migrants and visiting emissaries constantly are having use for it. Still, this was Africa. The majority of the home-grown were caramel-skinned to protect them from a burning sun characteristically towering high, so his guise was not to arouse suspicion or distrust. These humans were not overly complicated beings if one understood the patterns about them. As Samael did.

When the young prince boarded the saucer, a hologram control port projected itself after making an impression of his weight.

"This is really good," he commented on stepping off, but then catching that look in the merchant's eye. A look he usually got from most commoners. "You know, people don't know my father the way they think. When my father and I are no more custodians, we ferry like everyone else," he said pointing to the streets of the city that in seven days would no more be a burden. At least, not for another three years.

He was talking about the grounds. The grounds had walkways and floating trains coursing elevated runways. Runways connecting every home to a leisure park and every leisure park past a trading center, or trade port, like this one. It was all well connected; travelling both in and out the great tower all the way to the doorway. "You see these trains? These trains are overcrowded. And the elevators are a bore. So come. I'd like for you to meet my father. He's bound to see the usefulness of these— contraptions."

Eae bowed in appreciation, and still playing character, when he heard a whisper a long way away. They too were here. The others.

In the thronging crowd outside Babel, two cherubs blended evenly, walking the pathways and looking just like everyone else as they tried catching a train. It was

their telepathy that had given them away, so Eae agreed, easing his way into the child's private cabin quickly, a cabin full of his entourage, and a number of guards wielding light artillery. The cabin lifted itself, upon actuating, and they voyaged to the Heart of the Panther, the twenty third city up in the clouds, and the current administrative city; one of the three royal capitals of Babel. A city wealthy, industrious, and like the other capitals, uniquely frequented by record keepers. Record keepers like the ones he'd encountered earlier. The humans of course didn't know this. Still one thing stood out about this city being at the top of the great tower that put it under more watchful eyes than the other capitals of Babel—the doorway was stationed there. Always at the highest point of any city. The doorway not only made the Heart of the Panther, Babel's commercial center, but it also made it the most trafficked.

"So you're a merchant?" Keneji asked. There was a sparkle in the young royal's eyes. Eyes beaming like gemstones.

"Yes."

"How long have you been a merchant?"

"Three years," Eae lied.

"Three years! Which city?"

"Shimyr." His answer had piqued the child's curiosity.

"You are of Mesopotamia?—the great plain? You made this in Shimyr?" he inquired slowly and Eae leered at the young royal as their cabin made it past the fifth city. The

49

prince was obviously smitten by the merchant, and this flying contraption, but not when it came at the competitive price of outbidding the others.

"Yes," Eae answered pointedly.

"They make this in Shimyr?"

The prince's questions were becoming one too many, his thoughts ripe with envy, but they were still eighteen cities to the royal capital and Eae's much anticipated rendezvous with the monarch. So, not wanting to lose the young prince's interest before he got his chance with the governing monarch, he answered hesitantly. "No."

The son of the custodian grew quiet for a while, and thankfully so, watching Eae who had other things to watch. "Shimyr is a long way to fly," he remarked, finally changing subject. A remark that changed everything.

"What makes you say that?" Eae demurred, a glint in cherub's eye on picking up that subtle interjection in moods.

"Nothing," the young royal said, hiding behind a lie.

Eae prodded, "these saucers can't stand extended periods of flight. I hope you are not disappointed. Are you disappointed, your highness?"

"No," Keneji lied again, and Eae watched the child's vivacity drain away.

"Not the response you were hoping for?" Eae asked curiously, but the young royal shrugged off the remark.

Eae watched the teenager with askance, his eyes hinting red on gazing into the boy's soul, "you saw that!" he said surprisingly.

"No I didn't," the young prince retorted without having time to think.

"You see my wings," he said next.

"No! I didn't see anything," Keneji argued defensively. Not until he realized the merchant hadn't moved his lips. As in literally moved his lips.

He had to confess. "My father doesn't approve of me seeing things," he apologized, "but how are you doing that?"

A fortuitous turn of events as Eae stood to his feet. If anyone was to apologize, he was to be the one. "Tell me, boy, how many wings do you see?"

"All of them," spewed forth the flurried response. "Four wings."

"You're Nephilim," Eae remarked, levitating himself midair and towering over the prince. Keneji now getting to notice everyone, including his personal guards with him in the cabin, had succumbed to some kind of slumber.

"What's docs that mean?" he trembled under Eae's piercing gaze. Even as the cabin made its way past the 18th city. "Please don't kill me," Keneji pleaded, but that was the last thing he saw after the cherub burst in a red bolt of true light. It was also the last thing Keneji

"Come on! I know this is Babel. Yes. Agreed. My information might be off course by a couple of centuries, but I'm pretty sure i know what you did here. Or what you've done here. Simply I would like you to lead me to it, mein Gott. That is my request."

The seraph took a moment in scrutinizing them, before giving his reply. "I am only a record keeper, but I know all I need to know about the worth of your kind as i know about this place. I know about your greed for more and your lust for power. I know of all your wars and how you work tirelessly to divide yourselves no matter how many times you find yourselves together. I know all about you and your fuehrer, Herr Goering, but you will find no help here or what you're looking for."

The commandant did away with the fly whisk, "what is your meaning by that? We are the Aryan race. We will do whatever you ask. Just name it! We will offer no inconvenience. You might be surprised. All you need to do is point me where it is. Or which of you do I need to see to take me to this—to this—lost isle in the middle of the Atlantic," he retorted, a bit frustrated that neither his gun nor size could be of use.

"As i said, I am only a record keeper. It is the gate keeper you have to deal with. But i must warn you, Xan'el can be very dramatic. If you see him pop out of the woodwork, then he means to kill you."

gates. Everyone knows that," the fat custodian said behind a large mahogany table, but it didn't look like his son bought that. Or like he was going to drop this.

Jamidi of the Gulf sat in the heart of a massive red hall in a sculptured wooden throne of giant sphinxes, with illumination from the sun powering bulbs through yellow obsidian roofing. The diffused lights were awesome but wherever the natural lighting couldn't get to, the sonic bulbs took over, showcasing breathtaking intricate continental art across the walls.

"No. There is a seventh gate. You don't know there is a seventh because you're not supposed to know," Keneji replied, a dull glow in his eyes. There was something off about his teenage son, something bizarrely bold and no more as naïve. Virtually adult like. Perhaps there was some of him in there after all.

The custodian sat across from a bowl of bananas and oranges. So peeling off the bananas for a bite, he retired into the woodwork. A glamorous mahogany seat for a glamorous monarchy. "And where does this seventh gate lead if you're so assured," he retorted.

Keneji couldn't wait to see the look on his face when he said it. "Atlantis. Your haven of the gods," Keneji answered and the fat man ordered everyone out. Including the guards. This had been the moment Eac had been waiting for, but now he had a better idea.

Jamidi of the Gulf only spoke after everyone had filed out of the colossal chamber and into the lobby, "it's a myth! And even if there was any truth to it, it would be forbidden," he answered, watching the teenager strut himself before the table.

"Not to me," his son said smugly, even as the vivid impression of wings shadowed off a larger part of the carpeting. Jamidi wasn't supposed to see that, so Jamidi didn't see that.

"You don't seem your normal self to be telling me this. How are you so bold now as to mention it to me?" he asked pointedly. Yet, in the heat of the moment, stood breathless to his son's reply.

"Because I want to be the heir to the monarch who rules it all!"

"You mean Atlantis?—haven of gods?" he retorted with a simper. "Even your grandfather each time he prayed, saw that city as no joke. He wouldn't even let me mention it as a rule when I was your age, let alone conquer it!" When the monarch laughed however, he saw it was no joke. This boy, his son, was speaking seriously.

"6 cities," Keneji corrected. "You don't need to rule Atlantis, but you can rule the others. You can appoint your own custodians and not ever again relinquish power. Or share it. You can be greater than him; grandfather. You can make your own rules to supersede their rules. Be greater than all of them."

"You speak of this as if its remotely possible," he mentioned, watching his son beam, his eyes gleaming like opal in excitement. "There is a reason olden men call it the city of the gods. These are but rabid thoughts

brokered by an infantine sap unable to consider the cost—thoughts only to be fantasized about. Nothing more," he chided, but certainly buying into the idea. As a rush filled him.

"I know a way," Eae brokered. "I hear there are seven stones. All cut from one energy stone. Each stone stores and takes energy from the other until it makes a complete circle, perfect in balance, perfect in energy, save the stone that sits in the middle. This middle stone is connected to one and all stones. It controls the energy uniting the stones. These beings, your gods, call it the Mother Stone, almost as if all seven stones were still one. Anything that finds itself inside the circle of these stones is rendered powerless, even if it has the most power."

"And why would I take such a stone?" Jamidi of the Gulf asked, now serious, a tightening sensation in his gut.

"If you take the stone, you control the doorway. And with it, everything else. The city you call the city of the gods is in the middle of that circle because it's the seventh city, which is why you will find these gods powerless to stop you when you go and take it."

"And after I take it? What's to stop them from coming after me?"

"You'll see. They are only what we make them," Keneji sneered, and that was the clincher.

"I would swear I do not know you. How did you come by this, Keneji?" the fat man asked even as Keneji sauntered to reopen the doors.

"Shimyr," Eae brokered and watched Jamidi of the Gulf glower in rivalry. Humans were not overly complicated beings once you understood them.

"How much do they know?" the fat custodian inquired, trembling with excitement.

Keneji, or it could be said, Eae didn't answer that. The prince's silence was all that mattered.

"If anyone is to rule, it should be us. Not those blue-eyed twits."

Year of the black monarch, Haven of Atlantis, Bermud [8700BC]

All the gates were connected. The doorways linked all six cities to promote trade, communion, and science among the humans, but as fallout it tended to promote rivalry. In fact, a little rivalry was good. The Seraphim were fascinated by it because angels weren't known to put themselves before their kind. To the humans however, a little rivalry helped them better themselves. A strange thing.

The seventh gate was to keep an eye out. As well as monitor their advances. No human had ever entered

Atlantic city. No human ever needing to. Not until today when Jamidi of the Gulf came, the black monarch marching through the gate, weapon in hand, which in a new light posed quite the predicament because magic was disband in the city of angels. The island itself made a prison by the seraphs for cross-dimensional energy.

"The great Ariel listens to no one. In one possible future that will be her undoing," Bath Kol said heatedly. The seraph was not one to toy with her visions or prophecies.

"Is that so much a bad thing?" Samil said to her. His energy could be likened to the energy of the mother stone, giving a luminescent façade to the seraph's true form. He was of a short temperament, however. Not at all patient. "We destroyed what we had. They will do the same if we allow it so; if Samael is to rule, becoming this consuming horde that devours everything until it's too late. They are too young an existence to bear such burden."

"Give them a chance to dispute that."

"One day they will have their chance," he answered.

Both seraphs had been appointed to the Sixth Sanhedrin, and like all seraphs had six wings, but that was all they had in common, being different in almost every other way. Be it in thought. In appearance. In what you call sex. As well as ability.

The Sanhedrin of the Five and Seven were also present, their assembly a multiple array of what could be perceived by your sixth sense as essences. If you had any.

remembered of that millennium. And the many following after.

ou are not going to find what you came for," a voice boomed to all the officers from behind the columns, just one voice resonating as a choir of voices.

"Show yourselves—yourself," the commandant charged, as his compeers armed themselves.

And so out from on high, suspended over an air of nothing, came forth a being in plain glory, his form of a polished luster, and dark, just about as black as coal. Urel stood a sixth the height of the colonnades and his wings beat sashay.

"Fascinating! If i myself didn't see it, I wouldn't believe it. You are incredible! Which one of them are you?" the commandant inquired in awe, but the two remaining merchants fell prostrate in worship, praying and scared shitless.

"Diablo!" they confessed, but the commandant kicked them until they got to their feet.

"Get up you fools!"

Although they refused to look Urel in the eyes upon standing erect, the other Germans stood by speechlessly. And stood bravely. But all of them felt uneasy.

"I am Urel of the record keepers. And though I stand flattered by your fascination, the five of you should not have come here," he echoed at them.

The commandant bravely stepped forward, "We are only visitors, mein Gott. We're not five, but six humble visitors accompanied by three—i beg your pardon—two trusted boatmen," he responded respectfully, courteously taking off his officer's hat.

"Are you now?" Urel beamed at him, as every one of them took off their hats. And quickly too.

"I beg your indulgence for we've come a long way to go back empty-handed. Our fuehrer doesn't take kindly to failure—i don't know how i come to know this, or how things operate with you, but I'm quite certain you already know that. Just as you know the language I'm speaking to you now is not English, but my native tongue."

"Was woollen sie?" Urel boomed at him.

He tittered. "Ah! Danke schon. I'm sure you also know about the war? The war raging on out there—the war between us, we humans, so to speak. Yes. For the most part, we've come because of that! The fuehrer wants to unite this world, i mean our world, in a new world order, but as always, we humans don't see eye to eye. There are those who do not share in his dreams—a slight inconvenience. I, for one, am quite optimistic you will take kindly to my proposal being that you yourself—my meaning is your type sorry—have done this before. No?"

The seraph didn't speak back.

Everyone in the island could hear the uproar from a mile away. Only humans made such wanton noise. "The black monarch approaches. The human is here with his militia," Bath informed, a twisted smile almost dividing her face. The witch's energy could be likened to the moon's, giving the seraph a soft but esoteric polish.

"How is it possible?" Samil asked about the time he felt it. The time he felt them in the city.

"Perhaps today is that day."

There was nobody by the gates when Jamidi came through. This place was queer. But no sooner had he mentioned so, when they appeared out of thin air. Literally appearing out of thin air! That upset the monarch.

Keneji lied.

Samil looked at Bath with askance, "how does he know? Why would you keep this from me?"

"It is by your request I am here and remain here still," she rejoined in defense, "but how do you even expect me to see everything? When everyone, including you, keeps meddling with the future."

The monarch could see right to their bones when they came at them, through translucent muscles, and transparent flesh, almost a heavy blow to his resolve. He didn't know whether to retreat, or to hold his ground, either way there would be casualties.

When Urel made his presence known to Samil, he was quite certain the Sanhedrin already knew about the black monarch. What he was unsure about was their delay in any corresponding course of action. "They are not so easily moved. You should lift the band so we can defend our city," he'd suggested only for Bath Kol to glower at him.

"And which is the greater peril," she shot back. "Humans with their pricks? or breaking the seal? You shouldn't even be here. You're not old enough to tell us what to do."

When Jamidi and his militia were forced to defend themselves, the black monarch defended himself with no ordinary axe. One made by a sculptor and a physicist. One made by his kind. These beings bled a black viscous liquid when it tore through them, even as it scattered them, and in that brief moment the black monarch acknowledged that though his son may have failed to mention the entire truth, they were seldom gods. For no god bleeds.

Samil looked to the sorceress. "I do not know why you would lie to me, but I hope for our sakes you are not behind this," he warned, before stepping out of dimension to put an end to this. But Bath Kol wasn't one to be afraid of him. Ever since his appointment, she cared less and less for the Sanhedrin. Or what they were up to.

"Beware Samil," she said to him with that unvarying look of insouciance. "Know there is only darkness in his heart."

The haven of Atlantis was like no other haven as the island itself literally sat upon the seas; its obsidian rocks buoyed up by the mother stone—it's source. The sun reflected off everything and gave the whole island, what could be described as a glassy glimmer—and this insufferable blinding glare every now and then. It was what kept Jamidi from quickly putting an end to this fight. If it was a fight. "You're fragile beings. I'm just getting to know this now," the monarch announced as their assailants backed away, only for something to block out the sun.

Samil made his appearance before Jamidi. Unafraid of his weapons. Or militia. "You should not be here, Jamidi of the Gulf. Why are you here?" he spoke softly.

"You know me?"

"I know all of you."

"So what are you, people?" the black monarch demanded, a little fear in his voice on realizing these beings seemed to multiply in number each time he blinked.

"I can tell you do not want to be here, so why is it you are here?" the seraph asked in a telepathic whisper, and in what could have been a show of good faith seemed to have told the others to retreat. Or disappear to wherever it was they came from.

"The city is not what I expected. It lies bare and empty almost like a desert," the monarch mentioned, speaking in his primitive dialect.

"I cannot help you with what your human eyes see, Jamidi," the seraph replied, but calling the name Jamidi after the most eerie exchange or was it more of a clashing

of thoughts?—making the monarch realize, or was it suspect, this being was singling out his entire pedigree by the way he called his family name. It was more than a threat, even if Jamidi couldn't give voice to why he felt that way. "Leave. There is nothing for your kind here," Samil said.

The black monarch took a long glance at the gateway he came through, but he wasn't one to show fear. Or show his militia that he'd led them to an uncertain fate. "I'm told otherwise," he argued.

The monarch wasn't too complicated to figure out. "You are here for the stone?" Samil inferred, knowing the only thing complicated about this was the weapon the monarch wielded. It held two heads and could cut by him just pointing it. The humans supposedly intended it for leveling forests.

"I hear it is very useful."

"Leave now, without the stone, and I will spare your ignorance, Jamidi."

"Nah. We're beyond that now. You've just watched me cut down your kind. I may have even killed some. You're not just going to let me leave," he scoffed, and they both knew he spoke truth even if Samil appeared more in control, his voice gentle, even forgiving in tone. The seraph was livid with rage, even if the black monarch wasn't sure why he felt so certain about it. "These stones, whatever they are; they are more than gateways, aren't they?" he mentioned, but then hesitated before acting, "well, I've already started this."

The black monarch pointed his axe at Samil, but Urel appeared in plain glory stunning Jamidi and his militia for a moment, but buying just enough time to slip the seraph out of dimension. He'd already read the moment Jamidi made up his mind to see things through. But somehow it was almost as if the black monarch shared a window into Samil's thoughts. Somehow he knew Samil was never one to just let anything go.

The seraph ordered everyone off the island. The Sanhedrin too was to leave. "Someone has betrayed us," he said to Urel. "The human comes for the stone. They are frailer than we are."

"Then I request you let me summon her, if we can't lift the band?"

"No. The witch is right. We can't risk the dragons for this. We should end them once we're able to. All of them."

As always, his decisions had come rashly so the sorceress appeared in dimension. She wasn't as riled up as he was. Not having engaged herself in the overly brief skirmish. "If Jamidi takes the stone, you wouldn't need to. Unless you also fail to see that whoever it is behind their coming here has equally betrayed them," she informed.

"But we bear the greater risk. Those stones are a seal. Everything is undone if that seal breaks."

"Everything done was always meant to be undone," she answered tersely as they watched through dimension, watching the monarch and his militia tamper with the doorway.

"I fear everything Ariel's done is about to be undone."

"There isn't anything you can do about it. This day was always coming. You've just been too pig-headed to admit it to yourself."

With no one left to stop him, the black monarch put his hands into the gateway. As always, it rippled like water not letting his hands go, but this time, as how Keneji told him it should work, he refused to allow the doorway suck him into itself. Withstanding its tug with the backing of his militia, and after an almost insane spell of light, Jamidi of the Gulf found a stone in his hand. And a lot of static coursing through his body. It looked silver, glimmering lusciously in its own light. Just as it felt cold in his touch. And getting colder still. So cold the monarch hadn't complained, not even when his hand went numb, but something no longer felt right about the stone.

What the black monarch hadn't been told was that naming them stones was the closest to what humans could understand. In reality, all seven stones were only fragments of half a stone. Each half of this 'stone' connected universes, but together was called Crystal Eye, the eye linking dimensions. The best way in describing that kind of energy would be to call it cross dimensional; or likening it to dark matter, a source as broad as each universe itself, and ever consistent through time, which was the reason they used it as a portal of sorts. It wasn't any form of technology. Like most things, it just was. Just science foreign to earth. Or any dimension remotely close to it. This science was what ensured their salvation. One found out, or put together, by the ex-master and mind genius of their Sanhedrin, the saviour and destroyer of worlds, Sama-el. Its true intention, however, exceeded jumping space. The purpose of the mother stone was to channel, focus, or trap energy. In other words, and depending on whose hands it was in, it could be used for darker purposes. As a weapon. Or a prison. But humans hardly needed to know everything about anything before acting on it, which is why whoever had incited Jamidi to the stone clearly never told him the stone was what buoyed the island.

When the mother stone grew so cold as to split the monarch's hand frozen, the entire island lit up in a different kind of fire. A fire not remotely similar to earthly fire.

The seraphs watched the fools burn and drown in water. Still not one of them, aside the witch, took note of the similitude of a symbol, or its vestige, the fire had made as it consumed the island and sunk it, being that halycon fire in its burning was almost impossible to tell apart from water.

a Negro appeared to be by a polished plate set in stone; a very large plate highly placed among the tiers, almost like a shinning mirror, after Urel disappeared. He had red pointy eyes and looked more of a beast than a man when he walked up the columns and defied gravity. His muscles were bulging and strong, twice a man's. He was man yet beast, almost like a haunting by the slaves they sold, so the slave traders didn't wait to

begin running, though it seemed the Germans needed orders to run. In fact, the commandant couldn't figure whether to shoot at the cowards, or shoot at it, but started shooting when he watched it decapitate one of the slavers and swallowed the man whole—and that had been the man who had almost made the nearest exit. One of many exits. This Negro, or beast, or beastly Negro, moved on all fours and moved faster than a bullet. Perhaps he disappeared and reappeared, that seemed more likely because sometimes he was there and then not so there. The commandant watched this lucifugous creature pick off the runners. One by one. The most important thing he figured to do, was watch his back, for clearly it made an obsession of stalking the shadows and taking its kill from behind. When he was done being afraid, he made for the mirror, so he could have a clear view of the city, but on getting there he was paralyzed to go for his choice exit, realizing there was no longer a soul in the city. Nothing to serve as a distraction because everyone was simply gone. And by gone, the commandant didn't just mean dead because this being hadn't only eaten them, but cleaned up after them. Not a trace of their incursion into the forsaken city remained. No blood. No shells. No bodies. In fact, everything was back to the way it originally was. Even the illumination was out. So he waited, and waited for minutes on end, ready to offload his gun at anything that whisked by. Maybe it wasn't as invulnerable as it revealed itself to be. Though the more he waited, the more paralyzed he felt. That was until the commandant noticed the polished plate behind him made no reflection of him. Or of anything at all. He fingered it and it rippled like water, but the water didn't let his finger go. Or his hand.

Finally, he'd stumbled on the doorway. It made him snigger, at his own wit, finding it amusing not to have noticed the shiny plate in the first place. But it had felt as if someone pushed him because he suddenly found himself transported down to the fourth city underwater, drowning and unable to make it to the surface in time. He watched Urel floating two cities above, watching him drown. "It is as i said. You shouldn't have come," he remarked to the German. Telepathically.

The Fall of the first city came as a wakeup call. The new world was nothing like the one they left. This plane was not theirs. The rules were much different here. To survive as though their world never existed was just as stupid as leaving home in the first place. Or forgetting the war and the grudges that caused it. Aside the curse of dragons. To cultivate even a trifle of an existence here, would mean finding the proper guise outside the compromise of humans and wit of Nephilim. The entire exercise was not all waste though. The humans and their cultured civility could be used to an advantage. So the Sixth Sanhedrin reached a decision; each haven was not to be habitable, it was necessary to have the humans fan out, away from the doorways and knowledge of other forms of life for the most part—both terrestrial and extraterrestrial.

"Bath Kol will do as suggested. We all will. Though she doesn't fancy living as a refugee," Urel spoke, upon arriving, even as the seraph and cherub settled on the pinnacle of Babel, the great tower that had caused so

much change. "Nor does she desire acting as mother to these infants," he added, looking down at the multitudes thronging the tower of cities that climbed into the clouds.

"I hadn't realized we were at war with ourselves. It appears the humans are the ones who teach us now," Samil stated, watching Babel spread out below with more than curious eyes.

"Not us. Just Nephilim. They harbour a difference of opinion about the order of kin, you know that."

"Then it would mean we've been played right into their hands, with the decision we've reached. I sense the dragons are not all that we should fear."

"I do not think Bath is your traitor."

"Neither do I. The witch has a way of looking out for her own interests," Samil agreed, looking over his rejuvenated arm and foot the monarch had done a quick job of slicing, "but I'm going to appoint you to the Sanhedrin in her place," he said appreciatively.

"I am not of age. What will Bath think?"

"It's only by a thousand years. You're not pubescent anymore," Samil replied, "besides, i no longer can trust Bath, but I know I can trust you. I'm actually surprised your wings haven't started growing," he said and the cherub couldn't resist a smile. "One looks at this city and realizes it was not too long ago when we raised it up. How quickly they progress from all we've taught," he said, returning his attention to the Babelians and their great tower.

"They are puppets, amenable to whoever's willing to teach. What do you suggest we do with it?"

"Summon the Drangue."

"But...it's Samael's city?"

"All the more reason to destroy it," the seraph said eventually, so Urel lifted an amulet to the sun, casting the black shadow of a pentagram upon the entire city crowned with the numbers 6, 15, 23, 18, and 10 at the forks. "Take note of whomever visits after the city falls," he commanded, on watching the shadow highlight in red when the amulet hinted red and then disappear. As with the other cities, the seraph had been speaking literally. The cherub was to bury the city.

The sixth man was no German. He was no man either. It took Xanael one look to recognize that, before the visitor made the gatekeeper disappear. Or merged the gatekeeper with the city. Or trapped him in the body of passerine birds migrating past the edifice. Whichever the case, it didn't matter to Urel. With the urn weakened and Ariel returning, he'd figured it wasn't long before he showed up.

"As I said, you will not find what you're looking for, Samael."

"The last person who said that to me locked me away beneath a strange island for twelve hundred years," he remarked, his eyes a glint of red. And ambition, as he revealed his wings.

He could rightly smell fear in Urel; for his image was the splitting replica of one of the two sculptures mounted outside the city—save for the fact the Nephilim had grown a new pair of wings, having eight wings span out in glory.

"Impossible."

"No. Not impossible. Impossible is what they teach you not to understand."

"Nephilim!"

"Ah. That is what they call me, I see."

Dragonkind

angels and DRAGONS,
~dragonkind~

Vol 3

*D*ragons live off energy but only vast amounts from a giving source. And since your plane is just a big frozen tub of energy, they can survive forever in this world. Their nature hasn't changed. The best way to explain dragons to you will be for you to see them as magnets to energy, but unlike us who had to learn the art of garnering and channelling your energy to survive this world, they can absorb energy and just as easily bend it to will. Of the entire armada of dragons you have in this world however, there is a handful not like the others. We call them belamir meaning dragonkind. The reason being these intellectual creatures give off energy not their own, imitating and sucking on another life form to extend its own life. The best way to describe belamir to your reasoning will be to liken them to parasites—which is less than whole of what they truly are. These unyielding beings able to live off any energy source given that it is there. And given that we created you from genetically driven DNA and that your life is pure energy coined from the zygote of the first Adam to the last sperm of your kind, hopefully you understand.

The Kwasalis, Moshi, Kilimanjaro, NE Tanzania

He stormed into the modest house wiping the mud off his shoes, "if they are going to throw goatshit at the door, they should in the least feed the goats properly. Remind me why I took up this job again?" It was about 6.30pm.

The sun only just sunk beneath the horizon, winnowing a radiant pink defiant to the coming night time.

"Because these are your people, Benjamin Kwasali, and because we choose to retire here, and because we love our mountain," she replied all the way from the kitchenette, taking the oven mittens off and shoving the dough into the only other oven. As with most of the houses, the kitchenette was a simple wooden construction separate from the main house. In it, friendly females within the village had built her a mud oven. It was the only working oven being that was seldom electricity to power her modern oven. So she was eager to test it.

"So now you're baking for the entire village, are you Rebecca?" he asked when he got a whiff of it. The smell of muffins in the make was distant to the smell of shit he had in his hands. She came in through the doors of the in-house kitchen, passing her now obsolete electric oven— an equipment that stood in stark contrast to the new and empty house, as did her pale wrinkly old skin.

"No, unless you've forgotten we're having Elisha and his team over—then i thought it would be nice to whip up something for the children that come with the women to the treatment centre because one of them last week was particularly taken with my grubby bar, and you know this average aids worker seldom has those anymore," she said sauntering in for a balmy kiss and taking her apron off.

"It's going to rain soon," he remarked, trying to keep her clothes nowhere near the gloves he had on. "hujamboo."

"Hujamboo," she greeted back. "How was your day—and what's that smell?" she asked her swarthy, fish-lipped Wachagga expedition guide. Benjamin couldn't say so she spontaneously figured out the answer; walling up her eyes.

"Don't be upset."

"You don't need to apologize. It's been like what—3 years?" She pointed him to the porch where she'd moved the bin, and done a little rearranging of their humble accommodation.

"You know you shouldn't work too hard to make them like you," he suggested, delicately wrapping the dung in polyethylene paper and tossing it into the bin.

She smiled very briefly. "That's easy for you to say, you're chagga. You're not the one they call the cat-eyed witch—because I'm naturalized doesn't mean I look African," she replied, finding offense in his words.

"Is that so Becca Kwasali? You're every bit African to me. What more could they demand of you?" he cheered, flinging off the gloves and scooping her off her feet playfully into his arms. "I hope the women showed you how to use that antediluvian piece of jack or I fear all your hard work is going to waste."

"They did. The power is gone every time so all it needs is constant firewood," she retorted, "and aren't you and I getting too old for this—I mean you constantly squeezing me?"

"You don't mean that darling if you knew the horrible plans I had for you tonight. Just horrible," he winked at her and she held her mouth to a close.

"You bad man," she said as a clap of thunder rumbled. Without any warning, the rain began to fall and fall heavy by the pace of it.

"Hope you know a clay oven leaks like a basket? You're going to have sand for raisins in your muffins in no time," he chortled and she bat him with an arm, but it was too late to do anything about it. It was a rainstorm out there in no time; raining cats and dogs, as well as visitors after Elisha rapped on the door. The American guide was always with his mountain sack.

"Hujamboo! Anyone set for a little mountaineering?!" he cheered as they poured in, a team of two guides and two climbers—two Caucasian vacationers actually, one male and one female. They were soaking wet .The female Rebecca had come to know through the internet as Patrice, but the male she'd never met.

"Good evening to you too, Elisha. Sali. Patrice," she greeted fondly. "He's taking bath."

"Ouww, this house is remarkably less empty than I left it the last time," he teased, dropping the sack and stretching his legs across the bare floor, "but i'll say this. It smells delicious."

"Well thank you. I'm making—i was trying to make you guys something to eat. Nothing traditional of course," she said catching a look in Patrice's eye. Please find

somewhere to put your things. My husband and I are doing a little refurnishing as you can see. Your bedrooms upstairs, of course, are intact—"

"Oh thank you," Patrice responded kindly and with a thin voice, wringing her blouse free of water, so Rebecca sought helping the young female with her hair and the sack on her back. They all had mountain sacks.

"I see they still toss goat shit up your porch?" Sali asked. able to smell the shit beneath the bread. Sali's voice was deep and penetrating, as with all the locals of Moshi. Benjamin included. She sighed and the young man nodded. "At least they should feed the goats better. Some people are that small-minded, Mrs. Kwasali. Just ignore them."

"It's funny you said that," she said. He was warm and sweet and tall too. Too tall to be adolescent.

"I'm up for traditional or an ugali side dish. Hello! Name's David Johnson," the other Caucasian visitor extended his arm and introduced himself, being the only one she wasn't familiar with.

"Hello. I'm Rebecca. My husband will be your guide."

"I know. I hear he's the best—it's exciting," he lied just for conversation and Rebecca nodded because he was trying to be nice.

"I guess so; he does offer a new course up the hill, though if you ask me I think he's getting too old for the long hike up the mountain."

"It's going to be an exciting time," Elisha reassured her, "one of these days you should come up with us. It's quite an adventure."

"Me? Oh no."

There was a long silence as everyone waited awkwardly for Benjamin to come down.

"So where are you from, David?" Rebecca asked to fill the lull.

"Austria. I'm on safari, so I thought I might as well go with the whole package, you know. Mountaineering and all," he answered with a boff.

"I see."

Another odd silence. Patrice had a ring on.

"So, is she your wife?"

"O her?—No. Not at all. We just met," David answered showing his bare fingers.

"Oh sorry."

There was even more awkwardness, as the door creaked and more rain fell.

"I think i should whip all of you something to eat."

"That would be nice," they all said, more or less in speech, jumping at the chance to say something. Anything that would fill the lull. It wasn't as if they were going anywhere tonight.

412 feet above ground and by the fringe of a cliff, the high winds up on Kilimanjaro were posing a bit of problem to the team of climbers.

"Aren't the winds too strong? Can't we find somewhere to find shelter, it's dark already," David mentioned, trying to hold on to his mountain sack and keep the course.

"Yes but not here. It's too dangerous," Elisha answered as they trekked up the mountain path. "The winds will rip our tents if we make camp here."

"It's because of the rainstorm down there," Benjamin explained and pointed off the cliff. The men were speaking at the top of their voices. "It tends to ruffle the winds up a bit. Once we're clear through this pass, we should be out of it." He held Patrice by the hands as the path was slippery due to the ice that had sprinkled off the kibo accumulating along the way. They all were in full gear and the appropriate climbing irons but Sali still had to help with her mountain sack.

"It's monsoon. The winds are a valid concern," Sali mentioned.

"I know. We will find shelter soon," Benjamin answered, but then caught a frightened look in Patrice's eyes, "it's an easy climb if you just breathe evenly," he said at her and she bravely attempted a smile for him.

"So, what makes this mountain so special?" David asked from the back of the procession, seeking to distract his mind from the howling winds. He had Elisha to help him.

"For one, it's been named the highest free standing mountain," Benjamin hollered.

"Free standing what?"

"A free standing mountain! In other words, you're walking on the only real mountain in the world and not just Africa!" Benjamin answered smugly and beamed again at Patrice wanting to be sure she could smile back, and wanting her pale freezing face to flush pink. The guide was a bit sceptical she was suffering from high altitude pulmonary edema. If they were lucky, she wasn't.

"I've said this a thousand times, you'll run this business to the ground with all that touristic pile of crap," Elisha interrupted. "Nobody cares to hear that! Nobody wants to hear that! What people care to hear about are the little things."

"things like what?"

"Like this is the very mountain you met Rebecca—lucky bastard," Elisha retorted and they all laughed with friction, "see what i mean? Always gets them when i say that."

"Yes I met my wife on this mountain but that was the Arrow head route not this one," he confessed.

"All the same, it was a trip such as this, only for them to find out they both schooled at the same college in North

Dakota—my state. Couldn't keep all the warmth to yourself, could you?"

"Thank you again for the announcement, Eli. My wife and her friends from the action aid group wanted a more than traditional walk up the mountain, so that man kind of made it possible. But Rebecca couldn't climb properly because unlike this route that route required some climbing, so i had to help her out," he explained to Patrice and she sort of smiled back.

"I remember that route," Sali said, "i also remember he broke an arm and got us sanctioned—the entire crew," he said to David.

"The pin slipped, dumb fuck!" Elisha decried. "You were just a boy in the expedition, so what do you know of what transpired? And who's us? I didn't get you sanctioned because you are not part of the crew. Gosh!"

"I was learning the ropes, Mr. Elisha. You were scouting me out because i knew the route. Technically it's the same. I am part of the crew."

"Who told you that? You're the local. He does the climbing. I finance this thing. I was only scouting you out because you knew the legends about this place. You're my story teller," he scoffed and everyone snickered, "so why don't you just your job and tell them the story of the njaare bird you keep prattling on about instead of sticking that nose where it doesn't belong, hmm?"

"It's the origins of the name of the mountain i try to explain, not some story," Sali countered.

It seemed Elisha had pricked a nerve so David cut in, "I'd like to hear it. You speak well for a man educated inland."

"Oh please, he's just a yokel—they have cinemas here if you haven't noticed," the American scoffed and Benjamin signalled Elisha cool off a bit. Despite his reservations the boy was just a boy, Sali was indeed a part of the team—even if the young man was still in his twenties.

"My grandfather said the first explorer visiting Tanganyika that had attempted climbing this mountain had a problem forming words properly," Sali said to David.

"What's Tan-gan-yanika?"

"It's just the name of this place before it became a republic."

"Oh."

"Anyway, each time the old ones spoke of Kmilima, that is to say the mountain, he would say Kilima."

"I see."

"Yeh. It wasn't that much of a problem though, because basically they both meant the same thing."

"No—Kilima means hill. Kmilima means Mountain," Benjamin corrected from ahead and Sali shrugged it off.

"Yeh. Kind of. Where the confusion comes in is with the latter word, Jaro. You see originally when the chagga chiefs call it kmilimajaro meaning mountain of caravans,

he on the other hand would say Kilimanjaro, emphasizing an N before Jaro, which in all had a different meaning when he put it in writing— and also something else in Kwashili."

"Sounds complicated."

"Not so much. Njaro means greatness," David interfered, knowing a bit of Kwashili himself.

"Oh, okay. Then I suppose that's to be the proper name, mountain of greatness, 'cause to me mountain of caravans makes no sense."

Sali had turned to face the vacationer, but Elisha shoved him on, "face forward or it's a long way to fall, Mr. Apprentice. You've all people should know that."

"If you do not count the legend, yes," Sali answered as they continued the hike, "but it's also the reason you would buy into the confusion. For you see, he wasn't saying mountain of greatness as his following westerners thought he was saying. The chagga elders overlooked that small detail because he was a white man and because njaro also means white in Kiswahili as they barely understood each other at the time. In reality, no one got to know the legend of the caravans behind the mountain as was told."

Patrice seemed to pick a little interest, "so what is this legend with the caravans then?" she asked.

"it's kichagga. My grandfather heard it from his grandfather."

"So it sort of runs through the family?" David asked.

"Yes," Sali answered and couldn't wipe a smug smile off his face, "it's a story the oldest of the old ones remember. Some say even speaking of it is a curse so it's a story we don't normally share with foreigners around here," he mentioned and David skewed an eye.

"But that's why we pay him," Elisha interpolated and slapped Sali's mountain sack and equipment.

Sali shook Elisha's hands off his equipment, "Okay, okay! You don't want me to fall off. I'm carrying two bags."

"Sorry kid," Elisha mocked.

"The legend speaks of the kileman-njaare," he replied, "sounds the same but it means bird of prey. You see, to us, kileman means undefeatable—that which cannot be destroyed or overcome, and njaare means a bird or leopard. It's the best way to describe it. The truth is the old ones spoke of a giant bird and leopard like creature with that lives up on the mountain and swoops down at least twice a year to feed on the villages down there, at the foot of this mountain," he said, pointing off the cliff down at the twinkle of towns below. "They say its hunger was almost insatiable. Sometimes they offered worship and sacrifices to appease it."

"Did it work?" Patrice asked and Elisha revelled in their curiosity.

"Sometimes that worked. Most times it would just go ahead to raid the villages night and day for a fortnight,

fond of robbing caravans usually transporting men or beast and then disappear till the time it deemed fit to raid again."

"A bird leopard beast?" Patrice asked.

"Yes."

"Where is it now?"

"The Wachagga chiefs say it travelled a long way away, which is why no one has seen it, but there are those who believe it still lives up here in some cave in this mountain."

"Yes, people like his grandfather," Elisha mentioned and Sali repeated Elisha's words not realizing he was being mocked.

"Yes, people like my grandfather."

"Is it dead?" Patrice asked concernedly.

"No. My grandfather said they couldn't kill the creature because they couldn't catch it, and that they couldn't catch it because they couldn't see it."

"Well that doesn't sound right?" David retorted, much amused.

"That's what I heard, but that was until it stopped coming all together."

"Yeh. That's what he heard. The yokel doesn't make up the local legends," Elisha muttered disbelievingly to amuse

David and that was when Sali realized he was being made a jest and flung his face the other way.

"Auww, don't be upset," Elisha taunted.

"I liked the story."

"See? David likes your story."

"Really, it's just a community moonlight tale our fathers share to scare us and give us a kick," Benjamin said to Patrice on catching the same look he'd caught across her face only minutes ago. She'd taken the tale too seriously, probably because they were engaged high up in precarious winds. "My father used to tell me it was kilemanyaro, which is the name he's talking about—the destroyer of caravans, but none of it is real. If i had a son, I'd tell it to him too so forget about it," he cheered when they encountered a blockade after making the ankle pass 4,352 ft above ground.

locked?! How are we supposed to get over that thing?" David asked absolutely petrified by the heavy ice and snow that had fallen off the summit and cordoned off the rest of the cliff for a distance of five yards in the least.

"We have to," Benjamin replied promptly, already taking Patrice by the hand and starting her over the blockade.

"Can't we turn back?" he asked Elisha, hoping the American would be wee more agreeable.

"You must be joking. We just spent two days getting here. No, we can't turn back—that would be crazy," he chortled and pat David on the back. "Don't sweat it my man, it's just a little climbing—you'll enjoy it, money-back guarantee."

"Are you're telling me there's no other route?" he asked looking to Sali, for aside the heavy snow overlaying the path, there were slivers and chunks of ice in the snow that made the pass more difficult to wade through and every step uncertain. Yet, what bothered Benjamin was not what bothered the vacationer—it was David's first time mountain hiking and there were no seeming borders in the white snow as the snow indiscriminately swallowed up the mountain path whole. In other words, any misplaced step could mean anyone tumbling off the cliff.

Sali affirmed the negative by shaking his head and pointing to the summit, "going up this mountain is like going up a ladder—every way up is the only way down."

Despite Patrice being terrified of the winds, she bravely followed Benjamin into the snow to cross the blockade. "What many climbers mistake for fear is just the adrenaline kicking in," Benjamin whispered to her on noticing her eyes stray off him to the long fall down, "the secret is never to look down. Your body is designed to fall in line," he said, but immediately wished he could take back his use of the word fall as she angled her eyes at him like the miniature darts they were. She was terrified of the cliff and he tried to smile for her as they wade through the snow, making enough room for Sali to follow. Sali had her back, as he had sack, having to haul two mountain sacks across the blockade as she was too frightened to make it across herself.

"I'll do us a favour. Just hold on to my belt and step where I step," the American said to the European with an upstart attitude and brilliant teeth, before making his way through the snow and its underlying debris of ice and blocks. David followed.

The team waded steadily through the blockade, growing more confident with each step, and Benjamin had almost made it clear when Elisha was prating off about how long a drop his fall was and how little a time his cast was on— just enough for Patrice to take her eyes off Benjamin's lead for a second and her climbing irons gave way to a large chunk of debris in the snow. She nigh wrung her ankle, losing her footing, and almost her life if Sali hadn't caught her before anyone else could. The young man held on to her collar and her belt, but he himself stood in jeopardy because he hadn't strapped firm both mountain sacks.

 Elisha got to them before they plunged to their deaths. "Keep your belts secured," he muttered in the young man's ear and Sali nodded obediently, his heart beating wildly to a death that was not his. Patrice made it off the snow blockade near tears and embraced Benjamin tightly as well as the young man that saved her life. As would she of Elisha, if David hadn't slipped off something buried in the ice. The Austrian's plunge was swift off the cliff, taking Elisha down with him. He'd been holding on to the American's belt.

"We are dead," Sali uttered hands behind his head, their fall had caught them dumbfounded, so immediately he pounced on the blockade on a mission back down the mountain.

"Please, not through that thing again," Patrice begged but Benjamin couldn't say much. He just nudged her on, his hands reassuring her he would remain ever in her rear.

"We have to go after them."

"Oh my god! But they couldn't have survived that, could they?"

"I don't know."

The team of three had only just started back through the blockade when it happened again, and happened so fast—Patrice had barely skimmed the first obstacle when blood suffused the ice she trampled on. She jolted like a vibrator to the sight, only to make her way down the cliff the same way the others had. It was more than disconcerting, and not only due her fall because there was now the body of a little girl of Dravidian pigmentation now exposed in the snow, lacerated in two places by the hikers that had trampled upon it with wicked climbing irons.

The black child was hardly pubescent to say the least when they brought her in the eye of the storm. She lay flat on her back on a table all prepared for her with a body hard as stone and cold as ice.

"is she alive?" Rebecca asked pointedly and on the verge of panic.

"I don't know."

"Then why bring her here? To our house?"

"I didn't think. We didn't know what else to do."

"You should have driven her to a hospital or find someone who can—"

"Elisha's dead," he confessed and she embraced him solemnly.

"Oh dear! What happened?"

"He fell but i didn't see him fall. One minute he was with us, another minute all i heard was him falling below me—Sali says the Austrian slipped and they dropped off the mountain."

"The Austrian's dead? Jesus Christ!"

"Not just the Austrian. We lost the girl too. This trip is like a nightmare—it felt like she jumped. She just jumped," he said and Rebecca gaped. "We spent today scouring where we could for the bodies."

Rebecca stepped away, taking a step or two back, overwhelmed and gobsmacked.

"What's happened to them, or if anyone found them i can't say, but they couldn't have survived—they couldn't have survived that," he confessed, near tears.

"Oh my dear."

"Have you reported this?"

"No. I haven't. I can't. Ever since that thing with Elisha, the department of tourism withdrew our licensing. We run this without a license, you know that—"

"My god! Benjamin!" she slapped him and shoved him aside but he held on to her.

"I've been trying to get our license back. We've been trying since, you know that! You know Elisha's a pusher. He doesn't back down. Never before has this happened so I swear to you, he didn't expect this. We didn't expect this. You know me."

She embraced him so tightly, she couldn't help but cry with him, "I just want to kill you right now," she admitted then kissed him. It took them a while to stop crying and Rebecca looked to the girl on the table in their living space. "So what are we to do about the dead girl?"

"I don't know. She was naked when we found her, but it's been three days and she's still frozen. We found her buried under this weight of ice from the summit so I'm guessing something tragic happened up there and they left her."

"Who left her?"

"I don't know. Her companions or someone. Still, she's too young to be a climber."

"—of course, she hardly looks eight."

"That i know. I have my doubts. I had to bring her down myself in the end because Sali wouldn't even touch her."

"And how is Sali?" she asked.

"He's outside by the porch. He believes we're cursed and i agree. This trip is cursed."

She nudged him to go upstairs for a hot water bath and left to go talk to Sali only to find the young man soaking under the heavy monsoonal rain in the middle of slush the rains had made from dung and mud floating across the porch. Aside the fact he had caught a cold and was coughing chronically.

"Are you serious?" she barked at him and instructed him to get off the porch and quickly into the house for a warm bath, but he took to his heels and hightailed off their property. She couldn't believe her eyes on watching him run. She also couldn't believe her eyes when she returned into the house.

The little girl that lay upon her table had changed colour in every sense of the word—her skin was no longer as hard as a rock and of Dravidian pigmentation, rather it looked warm and tender now, and of pale Caucasian complexion. Except for the child's dark curly hair, the little girl looked exactly like her. She panicked and raced for her husband, but really didn't have to because Benjamin also raced down—half-naked and completely stunned.

"What is she?"

"I don't know."

Anje Erika Kwasali, Moshi, NE Tanzania. Present Day.

She'd been She'd been watching through the window of the very same house when he threw it. He didn't see her but he had her livid as a hornet when she stormed out the front door clad in her school uniform and a portentous aura. He took to his heels but she chased him down the street, despite missing a stocking—she was quite peculiar about these sorts of things.

"Erika!" Rebecca Kwasali called after her and quickly made her way out of the house, but the child was long gone by then. She had forgotten her school bag and the lunch box Rebecca had in hand. Rebecca retired to the house and suspired when she spotted it on the porch. It was too early to clean up such disgust but there it sat, more goat shit on the front porch.

"There you have it, Benjamin. She's just like you, she never listens. She's gone. How long is it going to take you to warm up the truck and finish up?"

Benjamin fondled for his keys and abandoned the oat and peanut meal, "you know it's an old truck, darling. The roads and dust are no good here," he said and grabbed a shirt to slip on. "Where is she?"

"I saw her chasing after a boy from her school. I think he threw goat shit at our house," she answered, picking up the matching leg of stocking by the window and handing

95

it to her husband. As well as the lunch box and her school bag. "I have to clean that up, but you get her to school. She's not like the others. Our daughter's more likely to get in trouble before she gets to school, you know that."

"Goat shit? I can't even remember the last time anyone's done that? We're back to the old days then," he replied and pecked her on the cheek as she grabbed a sponge and a paper bag of detergent. "Don't fret it. I will pick her up along the way, Mrs. Kwasali. She couldn't have gotten far," he assured her, before stepping out and jumping over the dung across the porch. "That's goat shit. Watch your nails," he cautioned her.

"You find my daughter," she cautioned him.

"I'd rather find the boy before Anje finds him," he chuckled and Rebecca looked crossed.

"I don't know how you laugh about your daughter just wandering off. This is serious Benjamin. There are wild leopards out there and her school is 5 miles away. You say there have been people missing you know—"

"Come on, darling, you're not that old. The only leopards i know are in the Serengeti. I lied because I took you there last week—ha! My dear gal, you need to see the look on your face right now."

"Get in the car!" she commanded him and Benjamin did. He took off chuckling with the truck engine chugging. The young Kwasali was probably a street or two down the road giving whoever it was a well-deserved beating. She was that strong.

He drove searching every dusty street until he made the express. Benjamin didn't find her. So the only thing on his mind till he got to her school was how unkindly Rebecca would react if he didn't find her there—at the Montessori teaching school. It wasn't a very big school and many of the pupils were still signing in when he got to the pretty reception room with picturesque stickers and drawings littering the walls. It was going to be a dumb question still he had to ask the slender dark skinned woman behind the desk, "I'm looking for my daughter—she's a special child?"

"And your daughter is?"

An overly weighty and heavily made up woman interrupted him, extending her hand, "Mr. Kwasali? How do you fair? How's the Mistress?"

"We're fine, mistress. Is my little girl here?"

"No, I don't remember seeing her. I would assume Erika was with you. You usually bring her in. Your daughter's a prize in this school. She tends to stand out. Is she not with you?" she asked rhetorically, but could see the senior was distraught and in no mood for sarcasm. She turned to the woman behind the desk. "Mr. Kwasali is the father of the half-caste girl schooling here. Her name's Anje Erika Kwasali. She's a senior student," she said but the slender lady seemed to decline by swivelling her head. Anje Kwasali's name remained unticked in the register and she showed it to the headmistress.

"Anje left home after a boy from your school. I think he made her angry. That's what Rebecca says."

"The only child that comes to this school from your part of town would be Eyalo Jnr. I'm pretty sure it's him, but the bus service usually picks him up. If that's the case, we could always wait to check the register? It might be she hopped on it," she proffered and Benjamin nodded discretely, "—you don't have to worry Mr. Kwasali, I'm sure she's alright. Children can be very creative when you least expect them to—" she said, but the slender lady interrupted her whilst pulling out a different register.

"The bus has already arrived. She isn't on it. I double checked."

"Then have you checked to see if Enay Eyalo was on it?" she snapped, grabbing the bus register from her, "she could have slipped by you unnoticed."

"He's not on it either."

She had her excused and led Benjamin to the open assembly at the heart of the school. The entire school was in the middle of taking the school anthem when they interrupted the assembly. A sea of children in different grades and their respective class teachers had gathered at the large assembly, but Benjamin was already sifting through the crowd for his daughter.

"Has any one of you seen Erika Kwasali today? In school i mean?" she asked, but the children stared blankly at them. Staring blankly at Benjamin. The senior's eyes were odd and hollow, showing signs of desperation as he sort through the many faces—two many faces Benjamin wanted to be his daughter's. The teachers watched him oddly and tried to keep as many children from him as they

possibly could, he seemed about to lose his mind and even looked too old to be her father. That thought had always been at the back of their minds since the very first day the Kwasali's enrolled her.

"And where is Enay Kareem Eyalo? If any of you have spotted anyone of them this morning, either here or somewhere else, please put a hand up. Or come forward. Children? Anyone?"

A child raised her hand from the crowd, but then pointed at a fair-skinned girl standing right behind Benjamin.

He couldn't be more relieved yet more angry, but all he could do was embrace her tightly. "You should never run away like that, Anje," he scolded, still she denied running away by shaking her head.

"So you didn't chase after a boy? –a boy from this school? Your mother says you did."

She denied it again so Benjamin let it go, but the headmistress approached her after he'd left to go get her things from inside the truck.

"So Erika, you are saying you haven't seen Enay Jnr. today is that it?"

Anje denied it again by a recognizable nod as her father handed over a lunch box and her school bag, only for him to discover there was nothing he could do about the odd leg of stocking Rebecca had him bring along.

"Thank you for the socks. Who gave it to her?" he asked the fat mistress because a matching pair was already on Anje's feet, and in pristine condition. He'd asked to thank any of the school teachers who'd spared his daughter the embarrassment of a missing stocking, but the mistress declined quite politely, and almost every other teacher he'd encountered on his way out—and all in the same courteous tone, so Benjamin left the premises not wanting to be perturbed by it because there was also no other way he could get the truth because of her condition.

Anje Erika Kwasali was a mute. She'd been that why since they found her.

For years, he'd watched the Kwasali house celebrate her self-coined birthday on the day they brought her in. Sali had kept his distance as he had kept his lips shut, but wasn't sure he could go through with the façade a third time. Not with people in the nearby villages going missing, especially on her birthdays.

Not many people knew that about Erika. Just him. And the twelve other vagrants he'd aroused into a drunken mob that fiery night, having the intention of burning the house down with their torches if the Kwasali didn't give her up. She was in her room in the upper floor. They could see that because the electricity was on, and so all the lights were up in the Kwasali house. The men watched Benjamin and Rebecca Kwasali take the last of the party decorations down when they hurled the first bottle right through one of the windows, smashing it.

They could see Erika's silhouette coming to the window in the upper floor, even as Benjamin came rushing out. He recognized Sali almost immediately from across the porch, despite the unkempt beards and gruff voice.

"She was dead when we found her, tell me you know that," Sali announced to the make-believe father as he approached.

"You're drunk. Just put the bottle down and come inside," Benjamin beseeched, approaching Sali delicately. He had a kitchen knife hidden behind him, just in case.

"Just tell me you know that!" Sali bellowed like a rhino and Benjamin concurred desperately.

"I know. But, you're drunk. You don't have to do anything rash," he said as Rebecca highlighted by the porch and he looked to the twelve surrounding his house. He sent her back inside the house. "You all put the bottles down and go home. I don't have to call the police!" he threatened the others.

"Call them! Let's tell them what we know," Sali rejoined and raised the bottle to Benjamin's face. "first, we are going to tell them that we killed three foreigners—we can't even find their bodies—so that everyone is going to know what we did. And then, we are going to tell them that she's not your daughter, so that everybody can know what she is. She's an abomination. Say it."

"Just calm down, Sali."

"Just say it!" Sali yelled back, mindless and agitated.

"No, let us talk about this. You don't want to hurt anybody, Sali. You're a sweet boy," Benjamin replied tenderly, but cautiously pushing the bottle away from his face.

"He always saw me as a boy. That's what he always saw me as—the fool. He was wrong. Yet he was your friend!" Sali barked at Benjamin replacing the bottle up in Benjamin's face.

"You're right. Elisha was my friend, but yours too. He respected you, even if he didn't show it. I know his death must have been hard for you. Even though you don't show it, but this is my family..."

Sali slammed the bottle against the ground and pointed the jagged shards of its neck at Benjamin, "—the thing is not your family, you must know that!" he threatened and Rebecca screamed at the top of her voice. Rebecca was upstairs with Anje in her arms. She'd barred all the windows and doors.

Benjamin backed away, "she is. Can't you see you're scaring her? You're scaring everyone."

Sali laughed and then vomited. It stunk of booze—the local type. "I will tell you now that I searched all the forest. I know you will believe me because I did and for two years, my friend. So ask me if I found them?"

"I don't know why you would go through the trou—"

"Ask me if I found them!" Sali snapped, his hands quivering with the broken bottle and Benjamin asked dutifully.

Sali laughed again. "No. There is nothing out there. Isn't that the answer you expect to hear? Truth is, you think me too mad and too young to take me seriously—like he did, but I see well, and better than the both of you if you do not see that thing you have there. Turn around. I bet they are buried behind your house, buried in ground like a dog buries bones. You're hoarding a monster. That thing is not your daughter," he said, but puked again and into the ground, just long enough for Benjamin to knock away the bottle and threaten Sali with the knife he'd hidden. Benjamin had even cut him just a little without having realized it. The other vagrants took to their heels, scrambling into the surrounding bushes off their property. Apparently, they didn't seem committed to his cause.

Benjamin took Sali in. The young man was wasting away to guilt and booze, now falling into a drunken stupor.

"You don't bring him in here!" Rebecca barked as she raced down the stairs. She was scared to her wits, but Anje didn't seem frightened though. She just stared at the man who'd intended to split her father's head open with a bottle.

"Just look at him! We haven't seen him in 3 years. Is this how you remember him?" Benjamin yelled back and dragged Sali to the couch, "help me lift him on this sofa."

Rebecca took a moment watching Sali, immobile and passed out, but after placing a lid on her fears, she decided to help lay him on the sofa. She took off his muddied shoes and smelly socks. Sali's breathing and clothes stunk worse than his feet so she dashed a second into the kitchen to fetch anything of use, even as Benjamin dashed upstairs to fetch a pillow to prevent him from choking over himself. But when she returned with an air spray, a mug from the top of the refrigerator, and ingredients to make a hot cup of tea, Sali was missing.

Benjamin came down stairs with a pillow and a blanket to find the same thing. He was there but a second ago. "Where is he?"

"I thought you took him upstairs. Please tell me you took him upstairs?"

Benjamin declined with a slow swivelling of the head.

"Where's Erika? Where is our daughter, Benjamin?" she panicked, already raising her voice. "Erika! Erika!!" she called, but Erika was no longer in the house.

Sali had left with her.

angels

DRAGONS,
~demons~

Demons Vol 4

There are a number of cherubim who do not believe what the seraphim preach—that your kind will balance out the war. They are not willing to take a chance with your kind, and who blames them? You are even frailer than we are. We know them as nephilim—the ones that oppose the natural order of things. The nephilim are beyond control and follow no rules in the new world. They only look to your kind for distraction and amusement. What bothers us, however, is that it helps no one's cause their numbers are steadily growing.

Obudu Cattle Ranch, Port Harcourt, East Nigeria

Jason remembers that first introduction very well, every moment still fresh in his mind of the day the man with the cleaved chin brushed them off. Nor could he forget the foreigner's carefree attitude after mother passed. It'd taken the notary five years to piece together a semblance of what his father looked like and ten more years to stumble upon him in a bar at Port Elizabeth— only to find the bloke not having aged a day and unconcerned to news of mother's ailing fate. He hadn't suspected anything out of the ordinary since mother always said father was of good genes—he had a chiselled frame, a vigour out of this world, and blue eyes that cut like gimlets. Mother was just a lonely gutala he'd met by a stroke of providence at that very bar twenty years ago and he let Jason figure that out all by himself. There was this pervasive confidence exuding from him. No. Jason didn't matter. Apparently, he never did.

The sound of animal husbandry woke the notary up.

"Where am i?"

"You are burnt to a crisp and all you ask is where you are?"

His entire body ached and felt like lead upon the bed.

"Am I dead?"

"You should be—my blood is coursing through your veins, but you're nephilim which is why it hasn't killed you yet."

Jason could literally smell flesh sizzling, and one sizzling beneath a caked and blackened exterior, but no sooner had he muscled to move his head when he noted it was his caked and blackened exterior. "It's hard for me to breathe," he said to the seraph and she beat her wings steadily in the damp hut to help the air go round. Between the cracks, his skin lit up like a furnace and water trickled out of it.

"It's because you're still burning. That's dragon's breath. The poison would work itself the next four days through your body if you're lucky," she answered succinctly and carved up a repetition of symbols into his torched hide with her fingers. It was a pair of S's crisscrossed serially and symmetrically across his broken flesh, and with every new pair his body seemed to close up the gaps and alleviate the burn. It was a slow and terribly painful process.

"Stop it. It burns," he confessed in agony and she leered at him.

In the least, she stopped flapping her wings and the air in the overly cramped undersized hut stopped circulating. She was naked, breastless, for she no longer felt the need to hide who she was, looking a frightening brown in the shade and in true form. He could see every one of her million nerves. "Do you still see him when you dream?" the seraph asked pointedly. She had a harrowing voice and a fearsome pinch as she put his broken body back together. The pain was muffling even as Jason was too exhausted to answer, yet she replied him anyway having read his telepathy, "I hadn't meant me."

"How do you—"

"It's annoying to know you're not going to stop asking me how i do that," she butt in mid-tense and in a condescending tone, "It's not me, but you. You're the one speaking to me, Jason."

"I didn't say—I don't remember telling you my name."

She leered at him again and his body seem to relax when he focused on her and away from the pain. In a way, he fell into a kind of anaesthesia. "I am the one keeping you alive," she said to him without actually speaking, so to speak. "We share blood. It takes me by surprise i 've come to share pekal matter with the likes of your kind," she added distastefully.

Jason nodded yes. A yes to pretend he understood whatever she was talking about. He didn't know how he was able to nod, but knew that in a way unfamiliar he'd actually nodded and it felt incredible. Almost like an out of body experience. "You agree but I'm not speaking of the blood I've just given you, Jason Ketuga. I'm speaking of why you see me and not him in your dreams ever since you were a boy," she retorted and used his own visions to explain herself. The seraph shared the vision of the man with the cleaved chin again, but this time Jason could see he had six wings spanning the entire bar and spanning out in glory. It looked like he was taken aback by how she could bend his mind and easily partake of his memories by just sitting there looking into his eyes, so she let him in on one more secret.

"I don't believe it," he protested and actually spoke out loud.

She answered him telepathically and quite succinctly too, "Your mother is already dead so you have your answer."

He went quite for an eternity, his thoughts not having a specific focus.

"I am looking for him because we're siblings. Until I found you i thought he was dead."

Jason's pain seemed to return and he cried out in agony in the small hut, despite the fact she'd healed his exterior and he was no longer charred black or steaming like a steak on barbecue. The new sensation burning in him wasn't due dragon's breath. In fact, a touch of his real skin was returning and his face was recognizable through the burns.

"Why would he keep it from me?"

"I seldom think that is the answer you are looking for?" the seraph asked back and watched him get on his feet. His one thought was heading for the airport.

"You're already here."

"That was a hotel pass, not a ticket—" he said to her having read the thoughts she threw at him.

"Still, I have saved you the trip and taken the liberty to bring you here."

"that ticket was five years ago, it doesn't mean anything," Jason retorted, opening the hut to find elephant grass fields tall as the shoulders extending as far as the eye could see. Even the rain was about to fall.

"Unless you know someplace else he would be, why would that make any difference?" Raphael replied and transfigured her semblance to that of a lady in a trench coat. She shoved Jason out of the hut into the cattle fields, and into the cold, as naked as a newborn baby.

Fort Nelson Air Base. Kimberley plateaux. South Africa.

mihr had an uncanny feel about her. Trixie could tell. She was literally developing cold feet even though she tried to hide herself and force the foot along. "You look terrible," Trixie inquired concernedly and the cherub huffed.

113

The Nelson air base was one in three air bases stationed on high ground, but different from the others and for many reasons Trixie hadn't the time to expound was a top secret facility, which was why the airbase couldn't be located on any map and why no visitors were allowed.

"This wound is interfering with my ability to conjure what I can."

"It's because you're in pain that is what we call it."

 The airstrip being active was more alive than ever before with pilots and their albatrosses either stationed, or taxing in line and coursing for the runaway. "Hey Trixie! There've been rumours you went static. Almost took you for KIA," a pilot shot at her as she ambled by the shadows of the fighter jets, having being blindsided from the marshals on vigilant inspection of the albatrosses and the fleet admiral up in the tower.

The airman had been up inspecting his craft with a face towel wrapped around his neck, but his gratuitously loud voice was enough to stir a second airman out of his cockpit and craft. This one had seeing goggles on. "Me, I knew she went rouge. Trixie's a stubborn bitch. Unlike you, she's too stubborn to die. Ain't that right, Trix?" he peered down at her and she attempted a smile, having intended to slip past the jets unnoticed.

"that's because you're a hard son of a bitch," the other teased and they laughed it off boisterously. "But seriously, what happened to you guys? I heard you were first to take on those suckers."

"Took a fall," she answered tersely.

"Makes sense."

"We downed one of those red motherfuckers anyways so count that as payback baby!"

"And more when we get back up there," the pilot with the towel pronounced excitedly.

"Wait. You're cleared to fly?" she asked.

"Yep. Everyone's cleared to fly with those motherfucking things out there still occupying our airspace."

"Both of you?" she asked again to be sure.

"What, you're deaf?—i said yea. Tonga taxis after Alba 4-1-1. I after this fucking rudder flexes out. FYI, Chief wants to see you," he said.

"What about?" she demanded impulsively and he snickered.

"What about—i'll remember that one. For one, how about i hint you the obvious you're not KIA?" the pilot in the cockpit said and pointed to the tail of the runway. There was a marshal headed their way. He seemed to have spotted her. "Chief needs to see you asap—and by asap, I mean now. And lose the beau. No visitors allowed on the strip you know that," he mentioned and watched her wall away her eyes, "—what? She save your life or something? Lose the beau."

"What beau?" the other pilot interjected, the one with the face towel in hand.

"You impolite motherfucker," came the insult. "Don't listen to this buffoon," he said to Trixie and her soft complexioned companion. Apparently, he'd seen Mihr standing beside her in denim overalls. He directed his goggles to his colleague in the other craft, "I had meant the lady by her. Really dude, it's not always cool to be rude," he retorted with a frown and Trixie looked to Mihr, but the cherub's foot was whiter than salt and bled in a growing pool across the tarmac. "Oh fuck! Am i leaking oil? I'm fucking leaking oil, man!" he pronounced on seeing a black fluid pool by his wheels.

"Hey, what's up with you? What the fuck are you talking about? What lady?" the airman with the face towel interrupted, genuinely calling the pilot with the goggles to his senses because there was no lady.

"You don't see that lady?" he asked but the other looked at him like he was just crazy, and simply turned to Trixie. "Yo, where's Charlie by the way?" he asked, but that was before both cockpits swung open and the two pilots found themselves rock hard against the tarmac blood-faced in a vicious liquid they couldn't see. Something had happened to Trixie to arouse such violence. Mihr could only watch Trixie get stronger while she was getting weaker, too weak to do anything by herself as the airman commandeered a jet and singlehandedly put the cherub in the passenger's seat—even before the air marshal could get to her or hinder the craft from taking off! The poison was obviously eating through Mihr, and now that they

shared life force things were only going to get worse with
Trixie.

Rio Muni, Gulf of Guinea, West Africa

ven though he had no color, his complexion was not
ordinary. It was dull and pale, as pale as a corpse, and
Ouriel feared his motives were forged of the same
ashen colour.

"You choose to stand in my way as you did him?" Samael
asked whilst watching the corpse of the German soldier
sink into the watery abyss of the cities underwater, but he
wasn't really asking. Samael was telling.

"You do not know me but i know you. I am Ouriel of the
record keepers and the 6th Sanhedrin. You shouldn't be
here, Samael," Ouriel stated, standing a sixth the height of
the colonnade, but sounding rightfully threatened because
Samael though choosing to appear small in visage had
eight wings. Not any of his kind had eight wings. Nor was
it natural because each pair spoke of a thousand years—
ten thousand one hundred and twelve human years to be
precise.

Samael laughed. "You are brave for one so young, but six?
Six is not a good number," he derided, casting vagrant
eyes about the city, eyes now silver with life, pulsating
with a glory in stark contrast to his pale cadaverous body.

"The last i remember this was my city," he expressed with
fondness.

"As it was Ariel's. It is yours no longer and will stay that way. As is evident, we have moved on."

"I haven't. I didn't see the suns for a long time before someone set me free—"

"I did but did so for another purpose. When I hadn't seen you emerge, I almost dismissed you for rumours. Still there was a part of me that realized all those years, if there was any truth to the rumour Ariel sealed you inside the stones, you will show yourself here someday. I didn't think it'd be today but it is as it is."

"Be careful when you state your purpose, or you will come to realize I am not of the order of kin," he smirked.

"I didn't bring you out to stir dissension," Ouriel retorted.

"Yet, here i am. I will have the stones."

"You most certainly will not," Ouriel barked at the father of the nephilim, but Samael was already misting like vapour defiantly past him. Ouriel's eyes flashed red with intent and the black angel reached out his huge hands to return Samael in place, but the nephilim misted through nonetheless—and easily too as Ouriel felt his very essence gain weight and stiffen. His body plunged into the water as his entire form took the visage of an iceberg, glass-like and frozen over.

"Contrary to the lies you were told, i am not the enemy. But the next time you, by your will, stand in my way, I will destroy you like you did him," Samael warned and moved to pick the silver doorway from its place at the peak of the

Babel. It shrivelled into his hands and the seraph entered into the waters flooding Babel. He melted away leaving Ouriel to the same fate he left the German—imprisoned and sinking to oblivion.

It was a kinder fate, drowning being only deadly to humans.

The Clear Water Hotel had a massive lobby and as expected it was crowded with intimidating Nigerians with curious eyes. They weren't ogling at Jason, that was sure. The lady leading him by the hand looked half-caste, probably indo-Aryan with succulent skin. She was a pretty one and led him by the hand to the reception desk. If they only knew what a grip she had. "If you can morph into anyone why not morph into someone less conspicuous?" Jason mentioned as they trudge through the throng with seldom enough private space to themselves.

"This form is easier for me," Raphael responded flatly without losing pace as she shoved through. In a way, she moved without friction almost as if her feet weren't touching the marbled flooring and Jason felt it. In fact, he could swear to it. How they could understand each other so freely was a very private matter and one equally frightening. On reaching the desk, she simply waltzed by the fat attendant in favour of the elevator but Jason paused a minute, "don't bother. He can't help," she interrupted his thoughts.

"It's still better we ask him. He works here."

"I already have," she cut in. "He's new. Same with the rest of the management. They are all of no help."

"Okay?" Jason responded doubtfully, trying to understand what she'd meant by that, only to turn around and find the fat man dazed by her, and dazed in every sense of the word.

"Eh? Where are we heading precisely?" he asked tersely, having an uneasy feeling about her. Or was it her uncanny ability to tamper with people's minds outside their consent?

"309 is on the presidential floor. That's what is on the ticket, isn't it?"

"I think I remember it being 209," Jason argued but the seraph could care less of what he thought.

"Then you've forgotten."

"No, i haven't," he shot back and quite frankly. "It's my memory. I think I remember I my own memory."

She leered at him as they got to the elevator and waited for it to open up. It dinged and surprisingly, amongst the multitude in the lobby, they were the only ones to walk into it. He stepped away from her as the machine shut the tiny box, already feeling claustrophobic to the nightmarish impressions of the woman in his bedroom and the nightmare of what could happen if she ever turned on him. He pushed on ten floors below hers and let the lift run up the floors without a word passing between them. Somewhere into nowhere, it jerked to a halt and

dinged open for a short rubber bellied man with thick beards an oversized t-shirt and shorts to saunter in and squeeze into the gap between them. He was with swag and with a cigarette that he didn't seem to mind smoking. By reflex he was to push down on the panel, but he ignored the buttons and let the equipment do its job.

"Hello. You know you're one sexy cocolet right just looking so helpless and sweet?" he mentioned to the lady in the sexy trench coat with a deep appealing voice, but she kept to herself remaining unpleasantly quiet. He turned to Jason, asking in a slow accent, "are you with her?"

"I don't understand what you mean."

"Halleluyah," he cheered and looked her over, refusing to put out his cigarette in the tiny space that boxed the three of them in.

"Name's Dede Ukoh, but you can call me Duke. My friend's call me duke," he said to her, drawing his cigarette in her face. "How long have you been around? You have family? Hope you're enjoying your stay in my city? It's your kind of weather this time of the year," he added, "—Indiana weather. It's like monsoon season," he slurred.

Rapheal looked into his eyes before looking away, and he smirked, "yeah I've been around. I travel a lot. In fact, my family runs this joint. We've been in the biz for years. Maybe i take you around the fun spots later this evening, what you say cocolet?"

Raphael didn't say anything.

"You don't talk much, do you? That's alright," he said and Jason sought to save the gentleman the unneeded attention. "Hey. Quit bugging her. I advise you let this one slide."

But he snappishly turned on Jason, "Oga! What's your problem, man? Was i talking to you? Don't touch me, abeg."

"Fine," Jason muttered, "hope you're ready for whatever you get."

The elevator dinged for the floor 201 – 210 but Jason couldn't get his conscience to step out of the elevator and leave the seraph alone with the unsuspecting male. He left anyway but took the stairs up after he figured the address shouldn't have been a corner suite.

"I don't think you know who I am so I'm going to give you this," the man said smugly, putting aside his smoke whilst punching in the key to his floor into the elevator panel out of boredom. He fumbled for something inside his loose pockets and pulled out a business card, lasciviously offering it to her inches from her breasts. "I'm an Ukoh. Governor's my uncle. Holla when you're ready to dump that dude," he said as the elevator opened up for 240 – 250 and he backed out of it, rudely gesturing to her a kiss and smirking. She patronized him by accepting the card, but it was to get it out of her face as she let it float out of the elevator. He quickly picked it up and floated the business card back in right before the doors slammed shut. She never even smiled at him.

The elevator popped open at floor 301 – 310 only for her to find Jason waiting by the door of it. He had a lost look about his face and sweat developing at the pits of his shirt, so she answered his question before he could ask or worry about the whereabouts of the previous occupant. "Your kind is what it is. It's never my intention to harm anyone," she confessed. Still, he looked at her with askance.

By the time they got to room 309 as she had seen it, she refused to enter but just lingered by the doorway staring at or staring through the door. Jason was about to knock when she turned away. "There's nothing we're looking for. He was never in there," she said whilst walking away and before Jason could make a fool of himself because the door sign had read Do Not Disturb. They returned to the elevator and since it was unknown to Jason where they were headed or what was now their current mission, he summoned the courage to ask, "Are we supposed to be heading somewhere?"

Raphael didn't answer, or maybe the cherub didn't have any answer, but when the elevator came, the doors swung open for the pair to find Dede Ukoh in it. "These Nigerians are quite resilient, aren't they?" Jason smirked, yet instead of picking up where he stopped Dede simply waltzed by them. There wasn't even a hint of recognition in the tall man's face.

"Did you see that?" Jason asked and Raphael didn't even let the lift travel down the floors when she grabbed the closing doors to a halt.

"I see it now," she answered him and he wasn't sure if he could ever get used to her snooping inside his head. She pried the doors open with her fingers just in time for pair to spot the governor's boisterous cousin make his way into 306 all alone.

"I hadn't meant we go after him. Or for you to damage the lift system," Jason confessed on noticing the hotel's security cams recording live footage. Raphael aimed her fingers at the twinkling green lights and all the cams sizzled from inside. The LED's stopped blinking. "They sleep now. Your kind easily forgets," she said to him.

They didn't have to sneak in. Her eyes glowered red and the automated lock to room 306 broke open all by itself. As anticipated, the governor's swagged up nephew was quite surprised to encounter them in his hotel room. He truly didn't recognize her; and had hardly recognized Jason other than a man he had ambled by in the hallway only moments ago, but not for long when she spoke a strange tongue at him and a tongue harsh on the lips. Right away, he took to the wall and ceiling architecture like an agama and violently came at them, he came at Jason actually, the timid one in the pair, just before a familiar symbol highlighted across his forehead. It'd been the same pair of S's she'd used to heal him earlier and that sealed the governor's nephew in place trapping it in midair.

"Fuck me! What is it? Don't tell me he is one of you too?" Jason asked, inundated by questions.

"He's nephilim—you call them demons," she said to him without mincing words. His following question was as obvious as the look on his face. She didn't need telepathy to figure it out, "yes, he's like you. You're a demon."

Jason looked to himself, speechless.

The jets had chased her across the border into Botswana, but after they left it was the Bostwanians that did the chasing. And if that wasn't bad enough, they had two missiles on their tail.

"It's a trap. There are too many of them. I can't shake them off!" Trixie announced though Mihr lay passed out in the back seat. "I doubt you'll get what you want. There's no way we can make it as far as Uganda like this," she confessed, still having a conversation with the sleeping cherub. For despite the fact that Mihr was asleep, the cherub's mind was very, very much awake and active too. "I'll try," Trixie said again and pushed the throttle to near stall, but that was when the missiles hit and the entire jet stalled. The angel had been able to launch the chaff in time to evade both missiles as Trixie's human eye was too slow to notice them, even so the jet plummeted to the stall with the Botswanians still firing at them. Trixie figured she had to balance the plane somehow. Or regain thrust if she could. Owing to the artistry of knowing what already was in each other's minds, their connection was inextricable, so when it suddenly felt like Mihr was no longer in the jet, Trixie panicked. There was this indefinite snap in the link and when she turned around, carefree of the fall, to inspect what was wrong, Trixie found Mihr in frightening form—an embodiment of an extremely intricate nervous network under a semi-material or was it a materializing ashen white colour with deadened and crumbling wings. It was then bullets hit the rouge SA Albatross. Amazingly, the jets refrained from pressing them after the Shashi as they went crashing and burning into the crocodile infested waters of the Limpopo. It wasn't long before the sound of helicopters roared over the crash site, however.

Swamp Tuli, River Limpopo, Southern Zimbabwe.

The porcelain wasn't her true self. That was clearly apparent when her fingers came off the moment Trixie tugged on them too harshly. Surprisingly, it was lighter than salt. "This isn't you? You don't have to say that to me again. What's going to happen to me if you die?" Trixie asked as she pulled Mihr to the cover of trees, away from the crash site, and away from the helicopters that came to inspect the crash. These helicopters were painted a different colour. It seemed they belonged to Mugabe's patrol so they had to be on the move. South Africa was on the list of nations Zimbabwe wasn't friends with, so it wouldn't be long before the entire swamp was on lock down and soldiers search every inch of the swamp seeking the pilot and his mission. Crocs aside.

"Possess me? What do you mean possess me?"

There was the sound of soldiers around the crash site, and since she was clad in military uniform, Trixie delicately picked up Mihr and moved into the woods. "Well I hope

you don't. Should I keep the fingers?" she asked, before picking up the fallen set.

Moving deftly and moving quickly, wading through the waters, they paced deeper and through the jungle. Yet despite twilight, and that she'd never been to this jungle before, Trixie had a clear direction where she was headed. Or was it more a leading she couldn't resist? But even if she couldn't explain each step, each step she took felt safer from the helicopters and their pursuers—so much so that in a matter of seconds, she couldn't hear them anymore. It was almost as if she was breezing through the swamp, avoiding the pits instinctively, and dissuading the glint-eyed crocodiles by just a stare from flint-hard eyes, and all this with Mihr across her back. It was an incredible feeling, an audacious and assertive feeling, but that was until she got to more solid footing and stumbled into the midst of people suffering from some unkind from of infection. It was a lost village. Or so it appeared. And she sort of recoiled to the sight of them. The entire villagers were walking like zombies and had lesions on their faces, boils on their torsos, and warts on their limbs.

"No, it's not okay because they are sick. I don't want to get sick," she stated to Mihr and put the cherub down, "any ideas because suddenly i don't know where else to go?"

"That's because I brought you here, Teresa of Springbok."

That voice wasn't Mihr's. The reason being the voice seemed to propagate itself into her subconscious self from a wooded house sitting at the heart of the dying village not too far away.

The wooded house was calling to her, from the looks of it.

"Yes but it's because you say so. Do you know who that is?" she asked Mihr as she backed the cherub and moved for the old log cabin. The wood was still wet to the other day's rain. "Who's Bath Kol?" she asked on getting to it, but decided to enter to get her answer.

It was a simple house with mats of oddly sick people and quite a young nanny for such an old bunch. She was intensely caramel skinned. "Lay her by the fire, Teresa," the nanny said to Trixie as she wringed dry a towel and placed it against the boils of one of the sick. The man screamed in agony and moaned as did the others when she was done. "These are my children," she explained, but that was in the place of a metaphor because many of her so called children were visibly older than her. The only furniture in the house was a small table strangely topped with meat, red, raw and just carved from an antelope, and a boiling cauldron on an open fire. The hot water in the cauldron, Teresa was soon to discover was not for the meat.

"How do you know me?" Trixie asked as the nanny dipped yet another towel into the boiling cauldron, wringed it dry, and laid it upon another agonizing soul. There was something off about the nanny, and that she realized from the nanny's complexion, for despite it being black as coal, her irises stood a luminescent blue.

She raised an eye as she sized Teresa up. "So you're the imprint?" she asked telepathically and rhetorically.

"How is this possible?"

But rather than give the airman a straight reply, she separated Trixie an arm's length from the porcelain cherub by just moving her eyes. Trixie looked stunned and looked to the sick people about the room. The nanny wasn't afraid to reveal she was different, Trixie understood that.

"You might look human but you still don't realize you're not yourself anymore," the nanny said to her pithily and turned to the porcelain cherub, immobile, and laid stiff by the fire, "Anyhow, I think I understand why you didn't tell her."

"Tell me what? What is she not telling me?" the airman asked but the nanny seemed to ignore the question to pick up a few of the red venison and toss it outside the house. Her hands were now all slimy and wet, yet she went ahead to rub the slime across Mihr's foot. But after drawing a mirror symbol of J's across the porcelain foot, that is.

She opened her hand to Trixie. The South African airman hadn't been asked a word, but pure instinct handed over the fingers she'd accidentally broken off. She'd just known that was what the nanny wanted.

"We do not imprint on your kind because you are weak and our pekal matter is stronger than you," she answered candidly as she affixed the fingers to the original owner.

"She was being stubborn when she made you but you share a source now so it doesn't matter."

"Share a source? What doesn't matter?"

"You being a part of us is a rare thing—her energy can't live alongside yours. It will displace your soul and consume your body at its slightest chance."

"Displace my soul? Consume my body? I don't understand."

The nanny never had to turn around to speak to Trixie, but somehow Trixie knew the strange woman did turn around and look her full in the face because her senses felt more than physical. They felt unreal; something newer and different from seeing, tasting, smelling or feeling. "If she no longer has a vessel, she will eat into you Teresa of Springbok. Or transform you into someone you don't want to be. Whatever way, it should kill you."

"But i am myself? I feel fine," Teresa argued but the nanny did something because the fire grew wild, burning out of control even as Mihr's porcelain form dissolved to a pale blue form.

"And what will you do about the marking on her forehead?" the nanny asked. She hadn't appeared afraid of the fire, so neither did Trixie.

"What marking?" Trixie asked back as two ethereal wings, Mihr's wings, spanned the entire length of the room.

"I don't know. I did what I had to because I must find the urn," came the intended response. Mihr had regained consciousness.

"If you are for Ariel, then you are of the order of kin. Imprinting on a human goes against everything you believe in, so know if the others find her you will lose her," the nanny said to Mihr and candidly. It was then they could hear the barking. Soldiers were approaching the lost village. "It will be another two days until you can get your life back and continue your search," she conjoined whilst showing them the back door.

"Thank you," Trixie spoke gratefully, and on their behalf, but that was when Bath Kol turned to them and said, referring to Trixie, "this one is different because her destiny is different. The imprint will fail. You will fall in love and she will kill you."

The blue eyed nanny had been very direct and Trixie stood speechless. Mihr couldn't transform into a more feasible form when they left, so she remained a soft blue with washed eyes just as her wings spanned the length of trees as they raced through the forest. Although the blue glow aided them in sorting their way through the rest of the jungle being dark to the intense forest cover, it could as well as serve them up as ducks and fix them into the crosshairs of every rifle because the blue was just too brilliant in the darkness to go unnoticed.

Fuck me! What do you mean a demon?"

"Stay away from him," Raphael warned and the notary genuinely backed away from Dede as she suspended the captive downside up and without actually touching him. "I recognize you," she said, turning her attention to the drifting cherub, his duplicate pair of wings she could see extensively.

"No, you do not. Not even when we stood in your face to kiss you," Dede taunted.

She ignored him but Jason did not. "Wait. I'm trying to get this. What you're trying to tell me by all this is that this is what it's like to be possessed? You can possess people?" he asked heatedly.

"There is one of us in there and one of you," came his answer.

"You possess people. How come you weren't able to tell he was well—different—when you met him? You should have been able to know right off the bat. I mean isn't there some dead giveaway to these things? Someway to tell? Someway to stop your kind from consuming it all?"

"It's magic. You cannot see what you do not know to be there," she answered succinctly and made a note for him to be quiet, "I tire of your questions," she spoke to him, without actually speaking this time, before directing her attention to her captive, "You're here because he's here. I want to know where he is. Where is he? I will not ask you again, nephilim," she threatened, holding his leg with his head close to the ground. She had resolved to dislodge

him clear off his host if he didn't answer her; that was how clear the pathway of communication stood between the three. It felt as though their minds were set on an open highway.

"I don't know," he answered quickly and his voice seemed to home in on the pair from all directions beneath.

"I know he's here. Summon him if you have to."

"Is that supposed to be some trick, governess? I can't summon your brother if I don't know where he is."

"Then why is it you are hiding your name?" she demanded, tipping him upside up before choking his neck to a close, her left hand imprinting across his neck as she grabbed him all the way away from where she stood.

"You're choking him," Jason said to her, but actually she'd never moved a muscle. At that very moment something just didn't right anymore—Dede struggled for air quickly going pallid under her grip while Jason attempted bolting for the door. Raphael released Dede, slammed the hotel door shut and slapped Jason to the wall telekinetically. She resumed the choke, gripping Jason's neck to a close with her right hand and cramping him against the wall. "Do you think you can escape me that easily. Tell me your name? I will not ask again?" she demanded from Jason.

Dede was now truly conscious and just stood there startled at the sight of the helpless Aryan lady pinning a man against the wall, and doing it remotely by just looking at him. She turned and scowled at Duke, peering into his eyes as she read his memories, "Why are you still here, Jamidi?" she threatened and the young man found his feet. Dede raced out of the hotel room without a second thought.

"Do not let him go. Terrible things will happen if you let that one go," he advised but she wasn't the one to listen to him.

"It is you who let him go. I am not of your order. I do not care for the nephilim," she retorted. "Now who are you? I will not ask you again."

"I am Eae," Jason answered tersely, sounding disappointed. "I'm thinking you'll want your human back, unhurt?"

"Yes. He is valuable to me."

"Then you shouldn't have let mine go. I have kept that one for close to a thousand years. Do you realize how hard it will be for me to have him again?"

"Your intentions do not concern me."

"If they don't, why do you surround yourself with this nephilim? Why should I give him back to you?"

"You will separate yourself from him or i will see to it that his body becomes your living hell," she commanded and he baulked because of her telepathy—she had shown him the memory of how she engraved her symbol into his body to keep the dragon's breath from tearing him apart. Today was only the first of the four days it would take the poison to do so.

The tides had turned. Eae had trapped himself. "It's been years since i saw your brother. I know is he frequents this place, four times the last year alone. Twice this year. That's all I know. You know you will have to promise me you will do me no harm if I give you back this vessel."

Raphael didn't have to answer, but Eae emerged from Jason as a brilliant red glint before disappearing completely, and suddenly Jason was flushing red to the choke she had on him. She released her grip before his throat gave way and he fell to the floor.

He appeared stunned and used. "What just happened?" he asked, looking dishevelled and a bit uncoordinated as his motor reflexes lagged behind. "It's like i had this epiphany."

"I warned you to stay away from him," she retorted.

"I didn't go near him, really. It's like I had this dream of my mother's old shack at port Elizabeth, but I could hear you talk, feel my pulse—smell my breath."

"It was not a dream. It was not a trance either."

"Then what was it?"

"A lie. Eae possessed your body. To do so he had to project your spirit elsewhere. Somewhere familiar to you."

"You mean astral projection? Wow! I didn't think such a thing was possible. Maybe I should be angry, but I must confess it felt great."

"Another lie. If you were human, your will would have been lost and you gone forever. Your will cannot be displaced so easily because you're not like the others. We can only possess your kind."

"Yes, I'm nephilim. You keep saying that like it's a bad thing."

She swung her strong feline bodacious self to him and spoke emphatically, "We do not think otherwise. I am of the Sanhedrin, nephilim. Normally i would strike you dead where you stand ."

Although she'd spoken fiercely, in some strange way Jason didn't feel intimidated by her. Actually, it was the first time he challenged her, "You've said that to me before. I'm guessing it's not so easy now on realizing we're related?" he retorted.

She ignored him of course, but as it appeared the notary was beginning to pick up a thing or two.

Demons

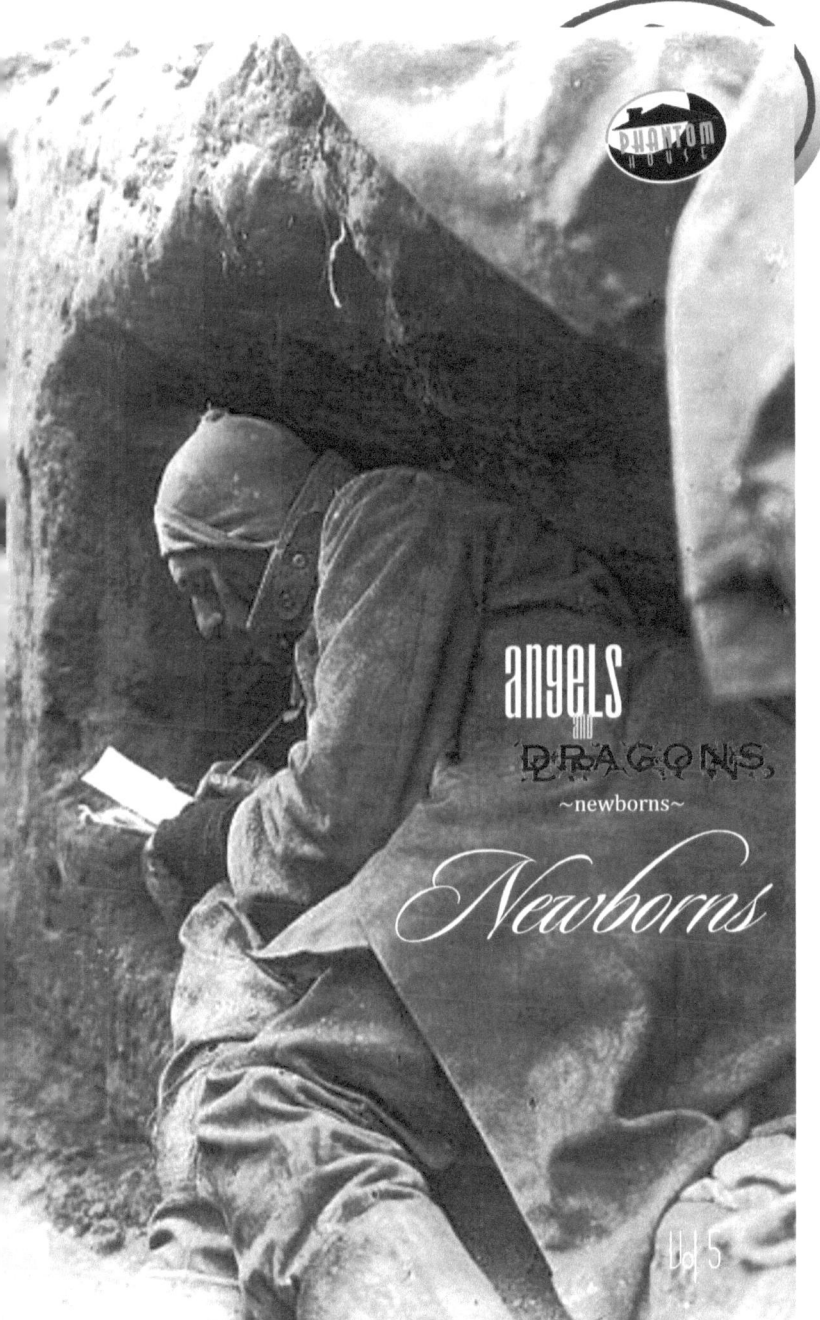

angels
and
DRAGONS,
~newborns~

Newborns

*Y*our strength is in numbers. What you can do as a group is the reason we fashioned you off an elixir and a glop of DNA taken from the best of what your frozen world could offer at the time. As you might have guessed, our kind cannot reproduce the way the dragons do. But you can. You see, we imprint on one another but seldom recreate a legacy every thousand years so our numbers have stayed that way since the first time. At such a rate, we will lose this war. Or worse, this world and the small haven we've made of it. With the exemption, of course, of siring your kind and making sure you share a similar fate in all this—which undeniably happens to be the reason behind your creation, if anyone was to let you in on the truth.

Dr. Guizot Sindehai & Brigadier General Lincoln Mabuto, Mobile Research Unit, Off Site Research Facility, Pretoria

*T*he spectacled biologist wasn't too sure it was a good idea being in the same room with it, but they had the red horn-tipped dragon sealed in a chamber behind protective glass. He put on his spectacles. There was something disconcerting yet reassuring at the way it stared at them through the one way glass, not blinking and never losing eye contact. Not even for a second.

"I can't believe its wings are distinctly made of cartilage? Makes one rethink our fossil finds."

"This is not Algiers, Dr. Sindehai. If you will not do it, I'll find someone willing to."

"But do you not see? Even that, that you see there, is refractory glass, still it sees us," the fair-skinned doctor said awed by the dragon's fiery eyes; a wealth of fibrous strands wreathed into golden irises that seemed to breathe along with it in ripples of red light. "How does it do that? Truly remarkable."

"What does that have to do with anything—?" the general retorted the Ph.D biolistics scholar in a prim lab coat. The general wasn't looking too stubby himself for his highly decorated uniform. In fact, aside the ever-present imprint of a scowl across his face, he was quite good looking by means of his pervasive sideburns.

"Everything," the doctor responded euphorically. "I have to get my readings. The implications of it are astounding. It changes what we think light is. Or what seeing is actually. I bet there is connecting tissue linking its nervous and sensory receptors—what i mean General is i think it more than sees us. I think it feels us too. Feels our bodies, our body heat, our position or possibly the voice of our thoughts—i dare not expound on that, but the odds are infinite. What a discovery!"

"—anything i require you to do, doctor," the brigadier continued the upended tense, growing intolerant of the leather-skinned sub-Saharan. "In fact you will have the time to expound on whatever you like, but will you do it is all i ask?"

"Do what?" the doctor asked back and the Brigadier leered at him, taking offense. "Oh that. If it works, certainly. The very first thing would be to—"

"It wouldn't work if you don't try it," the general cut in, losing every ounce of patience left in him and Dr. Sindehai caught the point. As well as the general's glare. So without ado, he let his team back in the lab before requesting they fill the chamber with an experimental dose of nitrous and sleeping gas sufficient to tame it or choke it to submission. But the gas did more than tame the fiery beast, it went ahead to immobilize it; though not its stare. It kept watching the doctor and the general from the floor of the chamber as a brave mechanism, the third of a number that had been damaged by hardened parts of its hide, clasped open its eyelids and injected a clear liquid into one even as it extracted a syringe full of black fluid from the other eye. The sub-Saharan doctor wasn't looking too confident with the process.

"What's the matter?" the general asked, now satisfied.

"The way it looks at us. It stares at us so cognitively. I can't get out of my mind that it hates us," he remarked and the general didn't look surprised.

"Unlike you, I don't expect the beast to like me, doctor. Feed me all your findings. I want to see a report by sunset," he snorted and walked out of the lab, which was but one of many mobile units about Pretoria, Capetown and Bloemfontein. He'd barely walked into his private cubicle when a hexagram with vivid prime numbers, 21, 7, 43, 37, 19 and 191 appeared across his work desk.

"The longer you wait, the harder it becomes," the apparition spoke but denied showing itself all together save for the shadowy impression of a man with wings cast against the walls by a tungsten lamp.

"I believe it was about a year ago I started believing in fairy tales. It was not too long ago if you remember i discovered your likes out there," he retorted and reclined into his chair, but not as much for wanting to rest his back as to secure a finger against the secret trigger built into his work desk. The small gun was experimental science he knew, but something in hand was better than nothing.

Zaphiel's shadowy impression of wings grew in contrast to the light bulb. "Put that away, general. I'm not here to hurt you. You have those things to do that," the cherub said, referring to the other area where Dr. Sindehai researched a dragon trapped behind bulletproof glass.

"Then what do you want because you've already made it clear to me what you want?"

"When will he have it? There's not much time."

"I'd love to say by sundown but you would know I'm lying so the truth is, the doctor has it. I made sure of that, but now that he has it, its property of the government so not to arouse suspicion you'll have to wait for me to push around the paperwork," the general lied and told the truth at the same time. It'd taken the Brigadier a year to cultivate the habit of twisting the truth, coming to figure these beings couldn't tell the difference to watered down truths the way they responded to wilful denial or an open conscience. "In any event, you should have it by week's

end. Though it does concern me what you intend to do
with it once you have it?" general Mabuto asked and
surprisingly the air in small cubicle grew hotter upon the
asking, despite conditioned air blowing through the vents.
His visitor had grown quiet or had left, but since he
couldn't be certain he kept his hand on the salt trigger.

"You need not be afraid of us, Mabuto. We've been around
for longer than you can imagine," Zaphiel replied after a
while.

"is that supposed to be comforting?"

"It is the nature of your kind to be suspicious of what you
do not understand. However all you need to do is say so
and I could always return you to the way i found you," the
cherub answered softly and the brigadier could sift the
pique in its enduring voice.

There was a polished kettle and a mug set by the
brigadier's table and in the skewed reflection of his image,
he caught a glimpse of the vicious scarring and third
degree burns that had once made up the greater part of
his face, but when he'd lifted his hand to crosscheck the
damage, his face was back to normal. It was no
coincidence. Neither was it his conscience. So even if he
had to be grateful, all the general could do was grunt. It
had done so on purpose for fear he'd forgotten.

"You'll have it as agreed," the general was forced to admit
and both the shadow against the walls and the heat in the
cubicle seemed to fade away upon his answer. It was hard
to believe they were any different from us, the brigadier

being once of the impression black mail was a solely human trait.

Ujai Sali, Mt Kilimanjaro, NE Tanzania

1000ft from the summit of Kilimanjaro, Sali opens his drunken eyes to find himself in the grip of black talons and flying towards a darkened cavern way on the other side of the mountain. He recognized the arrowhead route immediately, but not the winged creature flying him up the face of the mountain. It was always shielding itself whenever he grew conscious enough to look at it, yet had it not been for the vicious way it tossed him into the cave and against the rocks he would have caught a glimpse of it. When he came to however, he was in a dingy grotto lying by a kerosene lantern barely giving enough illumination to the semblance of Anje Kwasali asleep or pretending to be asleep across the sole entrance and exit. He picked up the small lantern to discover an ambuscade of idle fruit bats lining the roof of the grotto reacting timidly to the light. There was barely enough kerosene in it to keep the lantern burning through the night but what Sali couldn't reconcile was why he'd come to find a carpeting of sand in this dark cave up in the middle of nowhere for he was no stranger to the howling the winds made from outside the caves—they were a couple hundreds of feet up the mountain in the least, even if the cave stayed warm. He had the bats to thank for the heat, though it wasn't long before Sali noticed one of the lot feeding off his groin. He hadn't noticed it there before, but now that he did he wasn't too confident to slap it off, unsure of how the bat would react, or how the other bats would react to the

maltreatment as they weren't fruit bats. Lest to say,
whatever was blocking his exit because under the curious
examination of his lantern, it had not nearly as much the
semblance of a girl when pit against its resemblance to
the bats lining the cave. So he shook the bat off quietly,
stepping back and further away from the lady cloaked by
elusive velvety wings and putting her in the shadows with
every step, but that was till the time he knocked some
books over and the noise from the tumbling pile seemed
to echo forever. The creature stirred and appeared to turn
or twist nevertheless did nothing to suggest it had
awakened. The pile of books was one of many. So it was
all but conclusive to Sali the creature at the mouth of this
cave was Erika Anje Kwasali for the cave seemed to be her
library, or fortress, or maybe some kind of solitude for
despondent thoughts or guilt trips. He was still alive, yes,
yet he doubted he'd be able to negotiate with it. Whatever
mindful creature she was. As he sort through the books,
heading deeper and deeper into the grotto until the walls
could yield no more, Sali came to realize books were not
the only things Erika brought up here. She had fishing
gear, one he was certain Benjamin couldn't afford even if
he was protecting her. She had candles, drinking bottles,
rubber tires, masked dolls, a toolbox, but most common of
all—clothing and climbing gear, which was about the
same time he noticed a few bulges in the sand and noted
little of the gear in this hole was contemporary. Or intact!
Even as he pricks his leg against something sharp buried
shoddily in the sand.

Sali bleeds immediately, but when he hurriedly reaches
for the shard in his leg to inspect the injury, he pulls up a

femur—a human femur with bite holes! He drops the kerosene lantern almost immediately and the broken lantern starts a momentary fire in the cave—and a fire starting in the nick of time too, as he realized what was to be Anje Erika Kwasali was already behind him standing barely a yard away with wings mindful of the walls and golden irises that narrowed like a cat's. The creature was utterly expressionless save for the desire to sneak up on him.

Sali cursed and pointed the broken femur at her, "stay away! get back!" he threatened despite the fact she stood exceedingly smaller when compared to his size. Yet something about her let him know he was prey. In actual fact, he was holding it. She was as slender as bone and no longer the complexion of her former self, but had taken on a much darker complexion, a more caramel complexion like his. So save for the fact she charged at him when he pointed a femur dripping with blood at it, he could scarcely identify her. It was the face that had given the Kwasali away. Even if it had shrivelled to a caricature of itself.

What saved Sali in the face off was the growing screen of smoke between them, or was it the fire and bone, or the squeaking of bats exiting the cavern, for she quickly panicked and fled alongside the bats, even as the fire died out quicker than it started with the smoke clearing out minutes later. Sali couldn't stop his heart from racing. How he'd survived this night, he scarcely could recount. What was left now was climbing down the 2000ft mountain with little or no climbing gear. He was surely going to freeze or starve to death, if he'd forgotten how to

decode the complex puzzle of what once made scaling the arrowhead route so much fun.

The red horn-tipped dragon had stopped looking at him, so Dr. Sindehai thought to do what he felt humanely obliged to do—he lowers the dose of the experimental gas they'd been slipping into its chamber, having doubled the dose the past hour to keep the beast completely sedated. After that, it hadn't taken too long for the red dragon to wake up and when it did resume that daunting stare.

"What are you?" he whispered and stood by breathlessly watching it watch him through the glass. The second time it closed its eyes, it refused to open them. The doctor looked to his team of scientists, "What's wrong?" he asked them growing apprehensive but none of the scientists saw any reason for alarm.

"Nothing's wrong, sir," they answered back, looking to their computer readings and stats.

"No. Something's wrong," he muttered counting the seconds till the time the red beast would resuscitate its stare but it didn't.

It was not until they started having unsteadied to unusual vacillations in its breathing and bantam to flat cranial activity that they called to him, "something's definitely wrong, sir."

149

But everything had remained at a constant, so he was bemused by the lifeless creature inside the glass prison, unsure of what was going on. His apprehension grew, but it was until they asked him, "What do we do, sir?" that Dr. Sindehai remembered the gas pumping through the vents.

"We're killing it," he muttered, "shut it off. It's the gas. It's beginning to have a negative effect," he instructed and they shut the gas off, but even after they did its breathing waned to a flat with zero cranial activity.

"Is it dead?" they asked even as the leather-skinned sub-Saharan doctor stood speechless.

"It appears so."

So it lay dead a good five minutes and they were all but done packing up when all of a sudden their readings went wild and the red dragon burst through the roofing in a more than audible screech—according to the frequency and bandwidth scanners that is. Dr. Guizot Sindehai stood there laughing at himself as his team of scientists watched it soar to freedom among the clouds, "it was playing possum."

The other scientists were a bit apprehensive, "what do we tell the general? It wouldn't fit well for us if he discovers we set it free."

"Did you set it free?" he asked them rhetorically and they shrugged. "Then don't tell him," he announced in a light cheer, but that was until he noticed the shiny red glint in the sky headed right back at them, "it appears its coming back," he mentioned, but there was something about how

that red glint sparkled as it grew bigger that made all of them save the doctor bolt on impulse.

The red dragon screamed very loudly as it swooped over and spat its vicious liquid at the entire facility, first taking on the tanks and vehicles guarding the facility. It soon learned to avoid the nozzle of tanks and bend them into a hook to land them one into the other. Next, it moved on to each of the scientists working in that very room. What it did to each one was a little worse than the other picking them off in the five minutes of running they needed to get completely out of the vicinity and possible harm's way. And it did so to Dr. Sindehai's amazement, the horn-tipped dragon having far more acute foresight than what he'd originally proposed. It calculatedly intercepted and spat each one of them down by their most probable chance of escape, and not by who stood before it nor what attacked it. The doctor couldn't be certain if it could logically permute probability, or the even bolder assumption of differentiating variables, but the red beast was spot on with every attack and since he remained at the very heart of the complex, of all the others, he also realized it proposed he would be last—that is if his hypothesis was right. And surely when it was done immobilizing the tanks and liquidating everyone who'd been a part of his team into glob, it focused its vengeance on bringing down the entire structure by dismantling, liquefying, or hurling large enough rocks, at the complex with Dr. Sindehai in the middle of it all. The biolistics engineer stood there ready to die even before it buried him under a pile of rubble. It was truly an intelligent life form.

Forest of Many Faces, Tuli, Southern Zimbabwe.

ihr moved better through the forest, her form gliding through the woods in a luminescent blue glow, much unlike Trixie who suddenly lacked the inspiration, or was it desire, in heading nowhere. Aside the fact, metaphorically speaking, that something was eating into her because even if the airman felt nothing but ease and sincere relief at Mihr's well being, something uneasy in paradox mulishly remained. Most likely in her conscience, or was it her heart? She wasn't feeling herself so well that she could decide for sure.

"You're not confused, only torn between opinions. It doesn't have to be so," Mihr explained as she illuminated a path through the woods and deterred another crocodile lying in wait. The angel could distinguish her emotions clearly as well as Trixie's.

"Why does she speak that way?"

"A few of us are different—gifted from the rest of us."

"But i thought you were all gifted?"

"Being able to do this is not considered a gift by us," Mihr retorted telepathically, before sensing the huge cliff up ahead, yet not as much as she sensed what was coming behind them, which in a way was a fortunate spin of events—she not having Trixie laden about future events. "Bath Kol is not like the rest of us. Even some believe she

is up to par with Ariel, which is why what she sees is impossible to change even if it is subject to change."

"Ariel?—you've spoke of that name before. Is he the Ariel we're looking for?"

"Ariel's a woman," Mihr corrected tersely. "We do not marginalize our existence like it is in your nature."

"Oh," Mihr responded but there was more than one thought in the airman's head.

"I told you, it doesn't have to be that way," Mihr reiterated trying to put the airman at ease.

"You can't fucking contradict yourself and expect to keep me at ease, Mihr," Trixie muttered in rejoinder and at that moment the angel watched the green imprint recede from her forehead. Finally, her life force had sipped its way out of her completely and the witty old airman was back.

"You cannot kill me and I do not need to kill you. Do you feel better now Teresa of Springbok?" she asked sincerely. And strangely, without her smiling at Trixie, the young airman felt the imprint of a smile and the warmth of a hug upon herself.

"Yes, but that doesn't change what i want to know. I'm still curious."

"As is the nature of your kind but not everything can be put to words. It is a hard thing to explain time and destiny to a unilateral being."

"Try me," she persisted. Apparently, there would be no talking her down.

"If there is no time, there is no destiny," Mihr admitted concisely, but to help her understand better the cherub shared Trixie a vision in thought of their separate lives after they'd found the urn. "We don't have to be together for me to kill you, which is why once we've found Ariel, I will release you from this bind," she stated matter-of-factly.

"Your friend the nanny kind of gave me the impression that is a difficult thing to do. Funny thing is i don't even have a clue to why I'm asking now, only that her words are fucking beginning to get to me—"."

"In the least you have a chance. It is a good thing Bath intercepted us the way she did."

"Intercepted?

"Yes. That was me not you. We share a source now, so it's important you learn to not to confuse the two."

"Thank you for summing that up, Mihr."

"Be at rest that we perceive things differently from you. We have ample time before you fall in love, Teresa of Springbok," Mihr had said authoritatively but the airman in her private thoughts had humphed, "me, in love? How do you people-things fucking come by these suppositions?"

"We share a source. You should realize by now that I overhear your conversations in my head, Teresa of

Sprinbok," Mihr emphasized tersely, however Trixie's verbal communiqué had come out differently, "you're never going to call me Trixie, are you?" she asked and that was when a bullet slunk by and grazed one of the trees.

The cherub had kept it long hidden from the airman, so Mihr knew it wasn't going to be long before Trixie figured out only a curtain of trees on both sides separated them from a drop-dead cliff and the military might of a pressing army. It was either to be the devil or his cohorts. The choice was Mihr's.

Off Site Research Facility, Mobile Research Unit II, Bloemfontein. The Bloemfontein Mercenary Vehicle.

The general's plane had barely touched down an hour ago, yet he burst through traffic in Bloemfontein to make it to Unit II under 25 minutes—five of those minutes he had to secure trekking unmotorable terrain.

"Welcome Brigadier," Lieutenant Luwey Anderson said but Maj. Gnr. Mabuto shrugged off the handshake from the one-time family Dutchman the same way he shrugged mud off his boots.

"Tell me you've got something for me, lieutenant?" the Brigadier demanded on walking through the only curtains sealing off the entire perimeter, curtains made of nothing but plain nylon. "Is the site prepared?"

"More than prepared," Lieut. Anderson retorted trying to keep pace with the Brigadier general. Unlike the unit at Pretoria, the Bloemfontein unit was a strictly military facility and the entire facility was abuzz.

The general raised a brow, "we got our weapon?"

"You could say that," Lieut. Anderson chuckled even as they made their way through the plastic prop ups to the centre of the facility where some bare earth lay charged by an circle circumscribing a iron pentagram designed with numbers to each fork.

"Where is it? Did you move it?" the Brigadier inquired on noticing the heart of the pentagram stood barren.

"No, it's still there. I believe it feels uncomfortable having our eyes peer at it. Or any form of vision for that matter," the lieutenant responded, mindful of the charge and letting the general know to keep off the charged circle.

"So the numbers work?"

"Yes, Brigadier. As long as the gridiron remains charged, the thing isn't going anywhere," the lieutenant announced proudly so the general offered him a paper with 6 numbers on it.

"In that case i have a new set of numbers for you to try."

"Where did you...Brigadier, we've got researchers all around the world, researchers from Israel to India, searching for how to get these numbers. How did you come by this?" the lieutenant asked in disbelief and the general smirked.

"Just follow your orders."

"Certainly, but we'll need to a raise a whole new unit for this one."

"Make it an offshore facility this time. In fact, commandeer one of our aircraft carriers."

"Certainly."

"Where's your team?"

"Behind that window," the lieutenant said, pointing at a window in the structure a good height away from them even as the glint of an image appeared still occupying the heart of the barren circle. "They've been the ones testing every element known to man against this thing, so far only atomized sodium and chlorine, and their derivatives have some effect."

"Rock salt."

"Yes, general. Only the simplest hypotheses have proved true."

"It's not enough. We need something else."

"I know sir. You've said that before."

"You don't get it. They give us that. One of them gave us that. So fire anything at it, but get me something else that works!" the Brigadier boomed at the lieutenant, becoming flustered.

"We'll be working on it on the double, sir."

The general "So how about my gun?" he asked when the.

"This way general," the lieutenant said and led the way away from the rubber prison.

She chose the devil so hurried to the cliff even as it turned out to be an open area, but a helicopter beat them to it sealing off her chance for escape—being her chance because of the two, Trixie was the only person the soldiers could see.

"You are now in the custody of the Republic of Zimbabwe. Lift your hands in the air and stand away from the cliff!" the helicopter blared from its PA system as a soldier with a machinegun stood in the place of its safety door aside the rifle men coming through the woods.

Trixie did as was told but Mihr didn't. "What are you doing?" Trixie asked, looking to Mihr who opted to sing to the helicopter as she freely floated towards it.

"I hope you can ride this aircraft," she said in Trixie's head as she first made her way to the chopper's open doors and touched the gunner. A hazy evanescence came off him and the soldier fell off the craft limply even as she could hear the pilot through the PA, "Malik? Malik! What the fuck?" There was a tear in her eye. Not that Trixie could see it, but she could feel the tear almost as if it came down her own cheeks as Mihr drifted over to where the pilot sat and reached for him through the right window. At that moment, the air pilot could see her and screamed horribly into the PA even as he lost himself and control of the

aircraft over the cliff. Unfortunately, his scream drew attention because that was when the bullets came riding the air. The army in the bushes didn't stop to think and started shooting at Trixie because all they had seen was a failing helicopter, an unresponsive pilot, and a South African recon soldier watching the aircraft go down.

"Soldiers! Get me out of this place!"

"I can't teleport you. I can only teleport myself. It's why I need you to fly this thing," Mihr responded calmly but it sounded more of an apology.

"How can i fly it when I'm not in it?" Trixie retorted as she ran the edge of the cliff, but wasn't sure she could outrun the bullets, "they are shooting at me, Mihr."

"But i am! Just fly it," the cherub responded and at that moment Trixie understood what Mihr was getting at and the airman grabbed at non-existent steering wheels and tried putting the helicopter to balance. Bizarrely, it worked but that was when they heard a loud whistling sound powerful enough to push up a wind and rustles the leaves and trees.

"What was that?"

"Bath Kol. Get on the helicopter!" she warned because what stormed out of the bushes to take the army men by surprise looked more animal than human. They had heads and the upper body of hyenas overshadowing more human legs, bearing warts and lesions over all. The army shot at these beasts, even hacked some down with machetes, only for them to spring up with double the heads or double the arms they took down.

"Stop watching and get on it—those things can't differentiate who's who," Mihr remarked as the helicopter pulled up close enough and Trixie came to her senses. She jumped out to reach its skid even as one the creatures approached and lunged wildly at her, but it missed plunging to its death down the cliff as she held on.

"I recognize these things, but what are they?" she asked without asking as the airman clambered her way into the coach.

"It's because you've seen them before. Like you, they are humans," Mihr responded flying the chopper high and away. "Bath calls them gurengu— hyena men—weredogs. We call them demons."

"why would she keep demons?"

"for the eventuality she might need them someday."

"need them? Against us?" Trixe had questioned within her thoughts as the gurengu tore the soldiers apart mercilessly, but like everything nothing stayed hidden from Mihr too long .

"Against dragons," she corrected tastelessly, "but they are shady replications of Samael's true creation."

"What creation is that?"

"Humans. Samael created you."

hen Brigadier Mabuto returned because he got the distress call, he'd returned in the escort of the Bloemafestein Mercenary Vehicle, a concocted platoon of scallywag mercenaries with helicopters under the immutable leadership of a true lieutenant, and one loyal to the country. The brigadier's eyes were hollowed and narrowed, harrowed by the ruins and quiescence of what was once a functioning and expensive unit. There didn't seem to be any form of life in the entire perimeter as the other helicopters flew overhead, so they hovered over the vicinity searching for signs and survivors.

"I see why none of the soldiers made it out," Lieut. Luwey Anderson said, holding the chopper stationery above the site. The helicopters had come heavily armed. "It didn't leave anything standing. There's nothing here but ash, brigadier. That's one angry bird."

The brigadier was sitting by the passenger's side of the cockpit with a dead countenance. "See if you can find a place to land this thing," the brigadier instructed pithily.

"Already on it, general, though I can't say for sure. There's too much clutter."

"Just get this bird on the ground," he smacked when someone clambered out of the debris a good distance away.

"Who's that?" Lieut. Anderson asked squinting through the windshield to focus on the man in a haggard lab coat.

He seemed eager on his feet as he tried waving them down, and a soft glow warmed up the brigadier's countenance.

"That's Dr. Sindehai," the brigadier said coolly.

"but he's a bookie? To survive this? He must be one tough cookie."

"Have your boys pick him up quickly. I need him debriefed," the brigadier said and the lieutenant gave the order through the intercom so one of the helicopters hovered close enough to the scientist to throw him a rope ladder.

"He's not taking the rope," Lieut. Anderson stated when all the scientist did was flag them in the other direction, more towards the hills.

General Mabuto grabbed the built-in microphone to the PA system, "Take the rope, Dr. Sindehai!" the general threatened, his cheeks suffusing with life and expectation.

"I think he's trying to tell us something."

"Send someone down to pick up!" the general ordered the lieutenant impatiently, shunning the advise, before returning to reiterate himself forcefully through the PA. So just like before, the lieutenant relayed the command.

But the scientist was still waving his arms out, hand-signalling the general to quit the speakers and head towards the hills even when a soldier clambered down a rope ladder to pick the doctor up. Instead the brigadier like he was with warfare, asserted himself, insisting the

162

doctor get on the rope and refusing to let up. So much so that the lieutenant had to yank the brigadier to get him to listen, "I think he's trying to tell us something, sir. I think he wants us to leave him here?"

To his fortune, the brigadier didn't take offense and let it slide.

"No, not as much he wants us to get away," the brigadier corrected. "But i need him. I need him debriefed," he said and that was when a translucent vicious liquid struck down the helicopter before them from above.

"There it is! Gun it down," Brigadier Mabuto instructed but even as all the helicopters did so, they missed every shot. It took on the helicopters one by one and every missile they hurled at it, it dodged.

No lesser than a minute, the horn-tipped dragon flanked the general's chopper and was about to spit it out of the air when it caught a glimpse of the general's face and scowl through the glass. In an eerie gesture, it ignored attacking their chopper and went after the rest instead. But in that brief moment, the general caught the morbid epiphany of its intention, ""Let's get out of here!" he instructed Luwey and the lieutenant refused to cower from a fight.

"We can kill it. Just give me a minute."

"You can kill it the day i say you can! Just get us out of here, Lieutenant! That's a direct command," he admonished so the lieutenant veered the helicopter away from the fighting, but the dragon wouldn't let them leave which was apparent in the way it suspended everything else for a brief moment and came after them. It crippled the brigadier's helicopter by the crushing its tail rotor but for some god-forsaken reason kept it from crashing dangerously to the ground, causing only slight wreckage to the craft. It was at that time the missiles intercepted the beast and supposedly cooked it up real-good, according to the mercenaries through the intercom that is. The lieutenant unlocked his seatbelt immediately after the crash, and skirted around the broken chopper to help the general out of his side of the chopper because the brigadier had been knocked unconscious by the crash.

The burning dragon was slightly overhead, but even with the napalm torching it up, it spat directly at the other helicopters and attacked them with just the same vigour as before—some of the mercenaries rather ejecting themselves from the helicopters and falling directly into the precarious stone, steel, and ash debris below than die in the liquefying choppers. Yet it came after the survivors, able to tell precisely where they were beneath the chucks of debris and cognitively where and when to dip its claws or spew hot burning acid. Dr. Sindehai watched it kill off the entire platoon and then head for the general's chopper.

"Good god!" Anderson muttered after all he'd seen and when he noticed it coming for them. Unfortunately, the general's seatbelt had been mangled in place by the broken iron and equipment so he slipped out his semi-automatic and fired at the dragon to defend the brigadier and draw a line of defence, "motherfucker!!"

The red dragon screamed back at him even as it came swooping by, with burning napalm relentless in trying to make a crisp of its body. Yet it didn't seem to be bothered by the fire, or his bullets and shot wounds. It simply picked up the helicopter by the tail with the general half-unconscious and trapped inside it, and utilizing the entire craft as a weapon took a swing at the lieutenant before flying away with its plunder.

Doctor Sindehai came to the soldier's aid after the horn-tipped dragon had left with the chopper. He found Luwey Anderson in the cover of a rock but badly hurt. The soldier had no bones broken; only that he had fallen into a shard just to avoid being struck by a helicopter.

"How come you're still alive?" he asked, barely audibly as the doctor told him to remain quiet while trying to save his life and salve the bleeding with whatever was available around the debris.

"I think it has a thing for faces," he explained.

"Thank you, doctor...I've forgotten your name, doctor?"

"Guizot," he replied succinctly tying up the lieutenant's injury so that he let out a muffled scream.

"Thank you. You've just saved my life."

"Don't thank me. Not just yet. We still have to find some kind of phone under this rubble and get you help. I see you know me? What's your name?" the doctor inquired just to kick up a conversation and keep the soldier's eye open.

"Anderson," he said, walling up his eyes.

Anderson appeared to be a younger man than himself. He also didn't seem lucid. "Okay. Anderson! That's a good name," he said and slapped the lieutenant awake. "Just keep these eyes open, Anderson."

The lieutenant held a bloody hand to the doctor's soot-covered cheeks, "the brigadier...don't forget the brigadier..." he muttered but that was before passing out.

The doctor gave little time to thinking about it and focused his energy in finding a means out of there. For whatever the reason, he was lucky to be alive. The brigadier general on the other hand... well, he could as well assume the brigadier was dead. In fact, it would be a worse fate if he wasn't.

You can add to your library of
phantom house books.

GENERAL FICTION

THE BEDSIDE AND CAMP FIRE SERIES

Request for your favorite titles and our
newer books at your local bookshop or
visit your online retail bookstore.